The Best Day of His Life

A Novel by D.J. Hamlin

Northern Star Publishing, Minneapolis, Minnesota 2025

Northern Star Publishing, 2025

Series: Author D.J. Hamlin, The Best Day of His Life, Fiction: Young Adult, 1st Edition.

Paperback ISBN   13: 978-1-7332796-9-7

This novel is dedicated to Sarah, my wonderful wife who makes every day the Best Day of My Life.

Chapter One

It was as grand a Fourth of July parade as one could put on in the country's heartland. The Great Depression had gripped the United States for seven years now and it seemed that the people in small farm communities felt it the most. Pageantry was deemed important here because the average person on an average day felt less than average in self-worth. Pomp and circumstance seemed to lift the spirits of all, at least for a temporary moment in time.

The guest of honor was a surprise to all, including himself. Having wandered into this small midwestern enclave, Jonah really had no idea of what was going on. His arrival was by pure chance; he knew not a soul. The encounter with the police officer the day before had shook his thoughts considerably and now he was filled with bewilderment.

The parade assembled on the north side of town, just out of view of the main street. Jonah was taken to the end of the line and placed atop the last float. As he sat high up over everyone, he felt a wave of celebrity status rush over him. The people in front of him turned around to face him and they were calling out to him. The overzealous parade members were just the beginning of the show of affection that would be tossed his way when the whole group would move along the actual parade route.

Nobody explained to him why he was the guest of honor, but he gratefully accepted the position like he did with most of the things in his life. Jonah was a newfound wanderer who realized no significant place in the overwhelming world, but he felt ready to take on whatever the fortunes of fate could throw at him. The celebration just heightened his sense of being and belonging.

The participants turned around and began their slow, steady march on the route. As the lone police car leading the group turned on to Main Street the noise grew louder as the townspeople recognized the beginning of the event. The street was lined with three people deep on both sides and little kids were perched on the edge of the curb hoping to get heaps of attention and candy thrown at them from the marchers. A small but boisterous high school band followed the squad car and patriotic songs now filled the air. Jonah's float was now moving at a slow crawl and as he came into the view of the crowd, the cheering increased in intensity.

Smiling and waving to all he could see, the young man soon realized that his event and celebrity status was coming to an end. A moment of sadness reached his consciousness, but he pushed it to the back of his mind, determined to enjoy every last second of the celebration. These types of things did not come along every day, in fact during his lifetime fame had never come along.

With a final cheer from the crowd, he returned a broad smile and an enthusiastic wave as the destination of the parade came into sight. A beautiful little park with a pavilion sat off to the right and everyone entered a small parking area. Jonah had been here the day before when the policeman took him into custody. A proud smile crossed his face as he was helped off the wagon and led to picnic tables that held more food than he had ever seen. The delectable smell made his stomach suddenly growl in anticipation.

Led to the head of the largest table, he soon became aware of his fellow guests. All of them seemed to be prosperous despite the hard times that the country faced. Dressed in their Sunday best, Jonah felt out of place and it showed in his expression and actions. The people around him made him forget about his inadequacy as they treated him like their long-lost son. He thought to himself for a quick moment and concluded that this could be the best day of his life.

Serving plates piled high with food were brought to the table and he worked hard not to take too much, wolf it down, and look like a slob. As carefully as he could,

Jonah took his time and tried to show proper manners as he ate plate after plate. The aroma and taste were dynamic, by far the best food that he could recall ever having. There was no telling when his next meal would come along and so he took full advantage of all that was served. The banquet came to a slow but satisfying end with toasts to Jonah by the most prominent guests.

The group surrounded the guest of honor and led him to the small, three-sided pavilion in the middle of the park. Jonah found himself inside the strange structure with a shrouded window in front of him. The shutters that covered the window were made of wood and offered no view while closed and so the young man moved to open them. A hand reached out to stop his arm in mid-movement.

"You must not open the window until your admirers tell you too. They will chant your name and then when you feel the urge you can open both shutters and appease your subjects."

The old, weathered man was dressed in black and gave off an eerie vibe. Jonah knew enough to follow the directions, but he decided right then and there to stay away from the man for whom he didn't like. On each side of him were two people, a man and a woman, and they were allowed to stand in front of the glass windows on each side. Jonah was a little jealous; the man and woman could see the crowd and he could not. Both people smiled at him, bowed, and then slowly drifted out of the back side of the pavilion and out of view.

Jonah couldn't describe the feeling that suddenly permeated his brain but an alarm somewhere deep inside him went off. A feeling of instant dread made him almost lose his lunch and he felt that he had to see what was on the other side of the window. The crowd of citizens were cheering for him but he was given directions not to open the window until he was ready.

Deep down in his being he realized that he wasn't quite ready yet. Jonah stepped back slowly and moved to the side window where the girl had previously been to look out. His view through the glass pane revealed that the large group of townspeople were massed on the lawn and were ecstatic in their actions.

A colorful collage of energy and anticipation, men and women of all ages were grouped together as the celebration grew in intensity. Everyone was smiling and joyous, arms and voices raised in exultation. It seemed to Jonah that this was the biggest event of the year, bigger than Christmas or any other tradition!

This brought a smile and some relief to the young man. As his eyes carefully drifted further to his right, the middle of the gathering came into focus and Jonah saw a man about his age with people standing around him offering encouragement. This person seemed to be who the people were cheering for. The young man was holding a rifle and was aiming at the middle, wooden shutters.

Jonah panicked, turned, and took off in a sprint out of the back of the pavilion. He ran for his life, his legs moving faster than they ever had before. Running straight to stay out of the sightline of the crowd, he reached the edge of the clearing before anyone had a clue as to what was going on.

Up out of the small ditch and on to the gravel road he ran, out into the warm sunshine, and he heard a commotion brewing far behind him. A realization of being pursued overcame him and he veered to his left and across a small field while looking for cover.

It was suddenly right there in front of him, a large, wooded expanse and he entered it in a full sprint. The trees were spread far enough apart that he could run at full speed and as he faded into the darkness, he began to get emotional. Jonah pulled his thoughts together and continued his sprint for life with his survival instincts kicking in.

There were old, strange looking houses on both sides of him and this raised confusion because the dwellings looked dark and spooky; the buildings looked out of place. A thought that they might provide safety was quickly dashed by the idea that the people who were trying to kill him probably lived there.

The runner slowed down and looked behind him, hoping that he had gained some ground and precious time from his pursuers. The forest was quiet now and he struggled to catch his breath and calm his heartbeat.

Jonah walked at a quick pace, constantly looking back to check for pursuers and then ahead to find a hiding place to rest. The buildings were sparse now as he was deeper in the dark cover, and he saw a huge clump of bushes that reached taller than himself. It was a good place to stop and scout things out for a moment.

Jonah sat down on the cool ground in the middle of the brush and wiped his brow as he tried to slow his breathing, his mind racing as he struggled to comprehend what had just happened. None of it made sense to him but he was certain of one thing; he was being hunted.

Chapter Two

The Day Before

The day broke with a bright airiness that could only lift one's spirits to great heights. The shrill cry of braking wheels against steel rails startled the young man out of a deep slumber. Jonah breathed slowly, taking in the warmth of the fresh country air and he calculated that he was three quarters of the way back in the chain of noisy rail cars. Any threat of detection and harm from people on the train would come from far in front of him.

The train slowed to a crawl as it rounded a wide curve and a small but lively midwestern town came into view. Silently viewing the landscape and calculating how much time had gone by, Jonah surmised that he was still in America's heartland.

When the freight train finally came to a halt, Jonah jumped from the wooden floor of the boxcar to the ground with ease and walked into the wooded area beside the tracks. Hoping to avoid being detected, he crept toward the edge of the town. Up ahead appeared the small, ornate station where cargo would be unloaded and he quickly decided to veer in another direction and stay anonymous.

The young man reflected on how he had gotten into this situation. Turning eighteen had been somewhat traumatic for him because his birthday present was basically getting pushed off the family farm to earn for himself in the big world. America was deep into the Great Depression and times were tough; the home where he grew up was in danger of being lost to the local bank. Capable, sturdy, and smart, Jonah understood that his family needed him to go out and earn his keep to rescue them from despair. He was on a mission.

Hunger overtook his body and Jonah realized that it had been well over a day since he had eaten. A busy storefront diner was half a block up the main street and he planned to beg for his lunch.

Begging was better than paying at this point in his journey for he hoped that his money would hold out until he reached the produce fields and fruit groves of California. Midwesterners were well known for being generous souls and asking for assistance early could pay off later, increasing his odds of reaching the west coast.

He had seen poor souls beg for food back home and he always felt a degree of pity for them. To properly ask for a handout, Jonah knew he would have to approach the back door of the establishment. Charity was seldom given out at the front in view of paying customers and he felt embarrassed to have to ask for help. He knocked with a timid strike and a middle-aged woman with short, graying hair opened the worn screen door. He put on his best, yet humble smile.

"What can I do for you, young man?" she asked in a quiet voice that projected a motherly compassion.

"I was wondering if you could spare some scraps, some extra food?" he answered back with sincere respect.

"Certainly. You wait right here and I'll get you something to eat."

Jonah realized that he had been lucky to find this little restaurant with the caring lady and he said a silent thank you to his creator.

The woman reappeared after a minute or two with some leftover bread and roast beef scraps from the day before. This was sustenance that would keep him going for another day. Quantity of food overruled quality and because his journey was one built on survival, he would take whatever he was given as a gift.

"Thank you, Ma'am. This is very generous. God bless you." he answered with quiet reverence.

"You feel free to come back if you need more, you hear?"

Jonah nodded and moved off to an isolated area in the alleyway where the buildings provided cover from the sun. The temperature was climbing steadily and he started to sweat while eating. Figuring that it was going to be a scorching day, he knew that shade and water would be a necessity in addition to the food he had just acquired.

Attempting to remain anonymous, Jonah moved through the back streets of the quiet midwestern town and found a pleasantly shaded park with a cool, flowing stream. His ride into town had already departed and now he would have to wait for the next westbound freighter or possibly need to hitch a ride from a passing motorist on the highway. Traveling by train appealed to him more than the social situation of riding with someone in their vehicle. Jonah had no desire for conversation, just reliable transportation.

The gentle stream flowed along the far side of the expansive green triangle of grass and shrubbery and the tranquility grasped Jonah's attention. He was quite sure that he had never seen a park this beautiful.

Moving down an embankment, he dipped his hands into the cold brook and gently splashed water on his face to both clean up and cool off. The water was invigorating, and he couldn't help but shiver lightly and smile. Looking around, Jonah felt a little like he was back home.

The familiar town and surroundings suddenly brought on more feelings of homesickness. Wiping away a lone tear, he resolved to himself that he was a man and should toughen up. The feelings of loneliness faded away as he diverted his mind with plans for the next leg of his trip.

After an hour of contemplating his situation and future, he noticed an elderly man of important stature approaching from across the park. Jonah stayed put at the base of a giant oak tree and let the advancing stranger make the first move. He quickly assessed that this townsperson was law enforcement and as he got closer the uniform gave his purpose away.

"How are you doing, young man? What brings you to these parts?"

Jonah paused and chose his words carefully. He didn't want trouble.

"Sir, I'm just passing through on my way to California. I'm headed out there for work."

The older man smiled and nodded, breaking the tension. He had dealt with these people before.

"You're a long way from California, son. Where are you coming from?"

"Seymour, Indiana sir. Just passing through."

"I heard you met Jeannie at the café, huh?"

"Yes, sir. She was very generous...gave me something to eat."

The lawman kept a grandfatherly smile but added a tone of official duty to his voice.

"I'm glad. She's a fine woman, very hospitable. You're going to have to come with me though. You can't stay here."

Jonah looked around him and considered making a run for it. It was one thing to run from thieves, another to flee from law enforcement. He decided that going with the cop was a safer bet.

"But sir, I haven't done anything wrong. I'm just sitting here. Why are you taking me?"

The officer looked at the frightened young man and tried to calm the situation.

"You can't stay here. Come with me and you can get plenty to eat and a place to sleep before you move west. It will be a long journey and a short rest in town here will be of great help. California is a long, long way from where we are now. You will be fine, just follow me."

Ten minutes later, Jonah was sitting in a jail cell.

Chapter Three

The man with the rifle was not much more than a boy. Having just turned eighteen, there was an irony in play on this warm summer day. The designated assassin was named Hunter.

With his trusty hunting rifle aimed true to the window, his feelings bounced between fear and jubilation. The man on the other side would soon be his, a trophy for his entry into manhood, and the townspeople would forever recognize him as someone special.

The men in the town would admire him and give him the best opportunities they could afford. The women would see him as courageous and would be reminded of their own men in younger days. Most importantly to the young man was that all of the available girls his age would want him for their own. He would have his pick of the ladies and he had a particular one in mind. This event would seal the deal and win her heart.

The gathering was screaming and sounding cheers of encouragement at the front of the shelter and Hunter gazed around the crowd to absorb the attention, realizing that this could be the best day of his life. With a confident smile, he took aim at the window. When the shutters opened the trigger would be pulled and would signal up a whole new level of existence for Hunter in his community.

The cherrywood window covers stayed closed and he became puzzled. The crowd continued to carry on the crazed revelry, but he lowered the weapon slightly and locked eyes with his dad for a moment.

Both men were puzzled. The boisterous gathering was chanting the victim's name over and over, but the window never opened. The father held up his hands, the crowd quieted slightly, and he walked over to the window on his right. He looked through the window and turned in alarm, screaming that Jonah was gone.

Hunter lowered the rifle to his side and took off in a sprint around the pavilion. The young man to be executed was nowhere in sight, but he knew that the victim could not have gone far. Using his instincts, he ran straight and fast hoping to gain ground and catch up to his prey. Being larger in physical stature, Hunter struggled to run and he made it across the road and into the open field in twice the time it had taken Jonah.

He was an extraordinarily strong young man, handsome to most, but he wasn't keen on exercise. Profusely sweating and breathing with difficulty, he had to walk. As was the cultural custom, the big man knew had to catch the runner and the rules dictated that he couldn't have help from his colleagues. This was his hunt now and his hunt alone. What was to be the best day of his life had suddenly become his most disappointing.

****

After taking a few minutes to compose himself, Jonah stood up and brushed himself off as he stepped out from the cool, dark green brush. He moved very slowly with deliberate steps as he scanned for danger. He had no idea that he was part of a game, but he did realize that his life was in serious jeopardy and that he was at a considerable disadvantage. He also knew of no one that could help him and he had no knowledge of the area in which he was running. Jonah only understood that he was in the middle of nowhere, miles from anyplace he had ever been before.

Then he saw her. A slim young woman with flowing blonde hair was walking through a flowery meadow fifty yards away and he couldn't take his eyes off her. She looked more ghostly than human, yet more beautiful than the flowers she moved among.

Should I trust her and ask her for help?

He quickly contemplated his situation while measuring the level of danger in his mind and knew he needed assistance.

Hopeful that he had temporarily lost his pursuers, Jonah moved along the side of the woods that surrounded the peaceful opening where the vision of beauty walked. He got closer and then carefully emerged into the light. In a voice slightly louder than a whisper, he called to her.

"Hello. Can you help me?"

Thinking she was alone, the young beauty was startled despite the gentleness in his voice and she turned quickly toward the sound. She was brave, more so than most women her age and after a pause to identify where the voice came from, she moved toward Jonah. He held his finger up to his lips to signal quiet.

"Who are you and what do you want?" she whispered back after slowly drifting to within a few yards of him.

"I need help, they are trying to kill me."

The woman nodded and motioned him to the side of the clearing under the cover of the trees and darkness. She moved with stealth while surveying the area for danger. Jonah's eyes never left her and he decided right then and there that she was the most beautiful young lady he had ever seen. He trusted her instantly as his heart overruled the fear in his head. Out of the view of any danger their eyes met and the fear and tension of the situation dissolved.

"I can help you."

Chapter Four

Hunter was moving as fast as he could and he feared that he was losing ground in the chase, but he also knew that he had an advantage. No one would harbor the criminal and he knew every square mile of this territory. He had lived here his whole life. Regarding himself as a superb hunter and tracker, the big man knew that it was only a matter of time before he would bag his prey, drag it back to the town square, and celebrate with his people.

This practice of sacrifice was a long-standing tradition and there had only been one or two instances where a graduating senior did not pass it. Those who failed were forever scorned and looked upon as being unworthy of the status that the town bestowed on its people. Hunter was determined to avoid this fate. He needed the affirmation, acceptance, and in particular the affection of a certain young lady that he loved. Failure in this test was not an option.

I must do this and win over Dotsie.

Walking at a quiet but quick pace, the big man scanned left and right with his eyes. A human on the run would leave clues as to where he had passed and tracking him was probably easier than tracking the many deer that had been killed in seasons past. The patch of tall brush on his left caught his attention immediately.

Raising his trusty hunting rifle, Hunter moved upon the tall cover quickly and with care. No one was present, but it was easy to see that someone had been sitting there recently and the twigs of the long vegetation were disturbed on the back side of the bushes.

He was here! I'm onto him now...it won't be long before he is mine.

Looking up to scan the area, he reasoned that the logical direction of travel would have been to his left, further down the rough path that wove between large trees and disheveled greenery. Every so often a faint footprint of a boot would be partially visible. He had to assume that whoever left the print must have passed across the path recently. His confidence was growing with each stride and he began to smile as he moved further into the woods; he was on the right track and he anticipated catching up to his target.

Hunter suddenly moved out of the trees and on to the edge of a meadow as he surveilled the area for his prey. The big predator was careful to be quiet, yet he also realized that a noise might roust the other man and give him a chance to aim and fire. Scanning left to right with his rifle on his shoulder, he saw no one.

Jonah and the woman detected him in an instant and carefully retreated further into the darkness while keeping the man with the weapon in their view. The woman let out a quiet gasp and her expression gave way to her knowledge of who the hunter was. She knew Hunter well...she had known him since kindergarten at the small school in the middle of the town.

"Oh, no." she whispered with quiet apprehension.

"Follow me."

The couple moved deeper into the dark trees and began to move in a sprint away from the danger. When they were far away from the meadow and out of trouble, Jonah began to ask questions in an effort to understand his predicament.

"Who is he? Why is trying to kill me?"

The girl turned and tried to calm him.

"He's Hunter Carlyle. I graduated with him last June. He is completing his manhood training and killing you is his last task."

Shock and horror took over Jonah's expression as he wondered how he had wandered into this mess.

"Who are you?"

"I'm Dorothy Gravelle, my friends call me Dotsie. I live on the other side of the meadow where we met. The big question is who are you and how in the world did you stumble into our town?"

Jonah questioned to himself whether he could trust the young lady. He realized that he didn't have much of a choice as he was all alone in the world and one bullet from the teen assassin could end his life. The couple continued walking at a quick but quiet pace away from the meadow.

"I am Jonah Edwards. I'm traveling west to the coast...trying to get a new start. I come from Indiana. I jumped a train a couple of hundred miles back in Indianapolis and I got off here. I was hungry and looking for food and a place to rest. I walked into town and suddenly became something of a hero. Now I know why they all were friendly...I was supposed to be some kid's trophy."

His dejected attitude was evident and Dotsie felt sorry for him immediately.

"Hey, look at it this way. They didn't kill you and they won't if I can help it. It is all so archaic, so inhumane. The town has been doing this for many years and I think it goes back to my grandfather's generation. If you saw an old man in a black suit with an eerie manner, someone who would organize the whole mess, then you saw my grandfather. It's a cult, you know?"

Jonah's mind was still reeling as he turned around on the path to survey the situation and his pursuer. There was no sign of the kid with the rifle. The couple veered off further into the cover of the woods.

"How many people have they killed?"

Dotsie's expression was now dark as well. She took a moment to comprehend the question.

"Too many to count. Every 18 year old boy has to go through the process. They look for transients who pass through because no one will miss them or report them as gone. The influential men of the town have made the process into a celebration and all the town's idiots fawn over the group and worship them. It's a sick event run by sick people. I try to stay as far away from it as I can."

"I'm not going to make it out of this mess, am I?"

Dotsie turned to him and paused, measuring her response carefully. She realized that she wanted him to survive more than anything.

"You will be the first to get away and I am going to help you. Just trust me and do what I say. There will be people looking for us far and wide; this is not going to be easy but we will do it."

The young lady voiced her vow with conviction and Jonah realized that she was his only hope.

"So, what's next?" he inquired with a bit of dread in his low voice.

"We find you a place to hide and we bide our time. If we keep moving and stay away from the main roads and houses, we might have a pretty good chance. We also need to find you a weapon. I can get one from my house but if my dad sees it missing we could be in trouble. I know a place where you should be safe for tonight. Evading Hunter is going to be tough though, he's not going to stop until he finds you and kills you."

"How smart is this Hunter kid?"

Dotsie stopped and moved close, her eyes meeting Jonah's.

"He's smart enough to catch you if you make a mistake. He's betting on the fact that you have no idea of what is going on or where you are. That's where I come in. I can help you get out of this mess."

Jonah relaxed a little and took a few deep breaths to get his mind straightened out. The couple was moving at a steady pace and Dotsie knew how to evade their pursuer. She moved with grace and confidence and Jonah finally felt safe. Any worries about trusting her faded away quickly and he was taking a sudden liking to her in more than just a friendly way.

They moved quickly from the area and it became evident that Hunter was not going to find them any time soon. Dotsie led Jonah to an old barn on the outskirts of the town, over three miles from where they met and had last seen Hunter. The barn was part of an abandoned homestead that had seen much better days.

"This old building is pretty shabby, but it should do for the night. Don't leave here. I will bring you something to eat after dark and I will knock three times to let you know its me. Just sleep up in the loft and I'll be back later."

Jonah carefully opened a large, weathered door in need of paint and let his eyes adjust to the darkness as he entered the dilapidated structure.

"This thing looks like it could collapse at any moment. At least it's a place to hide and keep me safe."

Talking to himself gave him confidence and calmed his nerves as he carefully climbed the wooden ladder to the second level of the barn.

Jonah settled into a corner of the loft and thought about Dotsie some more. He wouldn't mind giving up his solitary life if it meant that she would join him. He smiled as he realized that he had a crush on the young lady that he first saw in the flowery meadow. Jonah hoped that he wasn't getting Dotsie in trouble. Suddenly, she was all he could think about.

The sun gave way to the dark coolness of the midwestern summer night and Jonah waited anxiously for his savior to come to him. Dotsie arrived well after sundown and she had an old bucket covered with a dishcloth. Inside was the leftovers that she smuggled from the dinner table. Despite the feast earlier in the day, Jonah was famished and the cold chicken and biscuits were devoured in the blink of an eye.

"Geez, slow down or you're going to hurt yourself!" Dotsie chuckled as Jonah ate all the food.

"Sorry, I guess I'm really hungry." He whispered back with embarrassment.

"That's ok, I'm just joshing you. You're kind of fun to pick on."

Dotsie put on a pretty smile and Jonah was smitten. He couldn't take his eyes off her and all he could do was blush and return a smile of his own. They spent a quiet moment looking into each other's eyes before the haunting, drawn out hoot of an old owl in the distance broke their magic moment.

"The bird sounds lonely." Jonah lamented as he sat back against the wall of the loft.

"He's probably calling for his lover." Dotsie whispered back with a knowing look toward him.

"I suppose you have a lover, right?" he questioned hesitantly, hoping for a negative answer.

"No. There is really no one around here that I like. I have known all these people forever and I am not fond of how they live and who they are. They are a sad, sick lot and I despise what they are doing to you. I am as free as a bird and do not need a thing from any of them."

"What about your family?" Jonah asked, hoping that she wouldn't ask about his. Curiosity forced the words out before he could stop himself.

"My family is dull. I am an only child and my dad and grandpa pretend to care about me. They really only care about their church friends and their cult in town. My dad doesn't speak to me much and my mom is gone, she passed away four years ago. I don't think anyone would miss me if I were gone."

Dotsie stopped talking and gazed at the floor, self-conscious of exposing her feelings to someone she had just met but suddenly seemed to care for.

"You don't think that they would really miss you?" Jonah quietly questioned, hoping to lighten the mood and give her hope.

"You don't know my dad. I seriously doubt if he would even know I am gone. I have left for days without him even knowing. I come here to get away, this is a quiet place that I like to call my own."

The young girl gestured with her arms wide as she surveyed the old but friendly structure. Although the wooden building had probably seen better days, there was a certain lived-in charm that both of them sensed.

Jonah changed the subject in a manner that he regretted.

"I suppose you had better get on your way, huh? We don't want people snooping around here looking for you and finding me. That wouldn't be fun."

Dotsie nodded quietly and rose from the worn floor of the loft. She took off her jacket that looked three sizes too large for her and gave it to Jonah.

"It might get a little chilly tonight, take this...it's an old jacket of my dad's. He won't miss it. I will be back sometime in the morning and we can make a run for it then. Sleep well."

Jonah took the coat, put it on, and buttoned up the front. Despite a musty smell, it felt nice and warm and he knew he would need it. His old coat was left in town by accident during the celebration. It was tattered and so worn out that he didn't mind losing it when he ran for his life.

"What do you mean by 'run for it'?" he asked as she turned away and started down the ladder to the ground level.

"We're going to get you out of here. If you're lucky I will take off also. You wouldn't mind that, would you...if I left with you?"

Her smile had a devilish quality and he laughed in a sly manner and nodded.

"You couldn't keep up with me!" he chided.

"Wanna bet?" she challenged.

They both laughed quietly and as Jonah settled down for an evening's sleep he smiled with thoughts of Dotsie running through his head.

Chapter Five

Hunter was frustrated and he kicked at the ground as he returned to the town and his home. A tear or two dropped from his eyes as he crossed Main Street in the dark, a single lamp guiding his way to his house a block away.

Damn it, why me? Why is it always me? Nothing ever works. I'm going to be the laughingstock of the town, everybody's going to hate me. They'll make fun of me and never forget that I failed. I'd be better off dead.

The young man made the last comment softly out loud but there was no evidence of truth in his voice. He wasn't really wishing he were dead, it was just a matter of speech and despair that he used much too often. His parents scolded him every time he said it, and he said it so often that after a while nobody paid attention.

I don't get it. I had his trail until the meadow out by Dotsie's house. That damned meadow screwed me up. Tomorrow I'm going back there, maybe Dotsie saw the man running or hiding. She could help me catch him. There is no way he could have gone far. Tomorrow I will catch him...I'm going to shoot him in the head and then it will all be over.

****

The knocking at the front door woke Dotsie from a deep sleep. She was dreaming and although she couldn't remember the details she knew it was good. She fought waking up until she heard the voices downstairs. Creeping to the landing at the top, she listened and tried to figure out what was going on.

"You know George...the guy took off in this direction and Hunter was on his tail. The guy is not getting away, no one does. If he gets out of the county and talks to the wrong people we could be in a hell of a lot of trouble, for sure."

A deep, gentle voice chimed in and she recognized it as her father's.

"Come on, Johnny, he's not getting away. The guy doesn't know the lay of the land, he doesn't know any people. He has no food or proper provisions for survival and he is not much more than a kid. I'll bet that we find him in a day or two at the most. The kid is probably out in the woods near here, cold and hungry. He will end up having to trust in someone around here and that will be his big mistake. He's a dead man, take my word for it. I just hope that Hunter tracks him down because if he fails, the town will never respect him."

There was a momentary pause and Dotsie made sure to keep still and quiet while eavesdropping on her dad and the sheriff.

"I suppose you're right George. They never get away. The guy has got no chance. I will do my best to help Hunter out…maybe do a little detective work without him knowing. Then I can guide him in the right direction."

The men moved to the kitchen for coffee and the voices were no longer clear. Dotsie knew what she was up against and now she had to formulate a plan to get Jonah across the county line and away from town forever. She dressed quickly while thinking and talking to herself and she began to make way out to the old barn.

The young woman snuck out the back door of the house and crossed her yard to the meadow. As she was rounding the corner of the outbuilding on the edge of her property she saw Hunter with his rifle.

"Hey Dotsie, how are you?"

His question gave away his shy interest in the beautiful girl. He had been in love with her since the first grade and now was embarrassed about his predicament. He hoped that she hadn't heard about his manhood training and failure.

Dotsie stopped and did her best to hide the alarm that shook her to the core. She didn't know what to say and the quiet seemed to last forever.

"Uh, hello...Hunter. What are you doing out here?"

The young man smiled to himself, relieved that she didn't seem to know about his failure.

"I'm actually looking for a friend who's lost. I think he was out this way. You didn't see a guy about our age, maybe about this tall, with blondish hair did you?"

He stretched his hands out in front of him to demonstrate the height of Jonah and he smiled as he hoped to convince her to help him out.

"No, Hunter, I haven't seen anybody out here in weeks. That's why I am so surprised to see you. No, I haven't seen anyone."

"Oh, too bad. Alright then, I guess I will keep moving on. It was nice to see you, Dotsie. Maybe we can go to a movie sometime? My treat?"

The young beauty smiled and nodded, hoping to lose the big lug quickly.

"That would be great, Hunter, let's do that sometime."

She turned and moved back around the building toward the safety of her backyard. She sat down on an old swing and waited for what seemed like an eternity until she knew that the assailant was gone. Then she took off out of the yard and across the meadow toward Jonah.

Hunter had been sitting on the far side of the meadow, tucked in amidst the elms, and he watched the beautiful young lady cross the meadow and disappear on edge to his left. Cradling his rifle with care, he followed her at a safe distance.

I wonder where she's going, there's nothing out this way. The town is back behind us. What in the world is she up to?

Off in the distance, the old barn came into view and everything began to make sense. He wasn't sure of the reason for her trip to this destination, but he had a good feeling about it. The best-case scenario would be Dotsie leading him to his prey. The worst-case scenario would be him meeting up with Dotsie in a secluded old barn. Either way he would be a winner and he almost wished on the second option.

Jonah had been up for a couple of hours and had been working on a plan. It was apparent that if he couldn't get away he would have to face his assailant and possibly fight for his life. This was a prospect that he didn't want to face. With no weapon, he was a goner.

Three knocks on the door signaled that Dotsie had arrived and he was eager to see her. The door creaked opened and within a moment he could hear her climbing the ladder to the loft.

"Jonah? Are you up there?" she called out softly.

"Hey Dotsie, I'm here. Come on up."

He smiled to himself about his dumb comment. Of course she was coming up, she was already three quarters of the way up the ladder.

"Hi. I'm glad you made it." he greeted with a warm smile.

Jonah moved to her and wrapped her in a tender embrace. Dotsie made no effort to move away, she seemed to melt right up against him. The embrace lasted longer than was customary and neither of them resisted. Then they heard the ladder creak.

Both turned to see Hunter standing near the top, looking over the edge with the rifle pointed at them.

"Don't move or I will kill both of you." the teen ordered as he ascended the last of the ladder's steps. Jonah and Dotsie stood frozen, focused on the weapon and its owner.

"You don't have to shoot both of us. It's me you want. Take me and leave her alone."

Jonah negotiated with a low, somber voice as he stepped away from Dotsie to protect her from the possibility of a gunshot. Hunter's eyes followed Jonah and a smile emerged on his face. The hunter had found his prey.

Dotsie turned slowly and then pulled her father's pistol from her coat. She fired and the bullet struck Hunter in the chest. The force of the shot pushed him off the edge of the loft and he fell backwards with a cry. Hitting the dirt floor with a loud thud, there was no sound that followed. Jonah ran to the edge and peeked over. The big kid was dead, crumpled in a twisted mass with blood emerging from his head and body.

"Oh my god, you killed him!" Jonah blurted out in shock. "I can't believe you shot him!"

Dotsie sank to her knees and began sobbing with the realization of what she had just done. She laid the pistol on the floor and cried louder. Jonah rushed to her and held her gently while she broke down. He did his best to help her regain her composure as he knew they would have to do something before anyone found them.

The body was too heavy for one person to lift and Jonah had to ask for help. He feared that Dotsie would fall apart with emotion if she saw the dead kid, the person she had killed.

"Dots, I hate to ask but could you help me move the body?"

She backed down the ladder without looking at Hunter and when she pivoted to the ground she couldn't help but glance.

"Oh my god!" she cried as she fell to the dirt floor in anguish.

The dead boy lay on his back, his neck broken and twisted in an unnatural way. His eyes were staring up in permanent alarm, gray with death. Blood was seeping from his side and was mixing with the dirt into a muddy mess.

Jonah knelt next to Dotsie and shielded her from the grotesque view. He reached out and gently wrapped his arm around her as she shook with fear and shock.

"It's ok, Dotsie, it's ok. You had to do it...we had to do it. He was going to kill me. You saved my life, do you understand? You saved my life."

She didn't say a word as she rose to her feet. Staring straight ahead, she made her way to the far corner of the barn and pulled an old tarp off a rusted plow.

"We can wrap him in this." she declared quietly.

Jonah took the tarp and placed the body on it, wrapping both sides up to completely cover the corpse. After placing an old spade shovel on top of the body, they both grabbed a corner and dragged the dead boy fifty yards to the edge of the woods.

Shoveling for what seemed like an eternity, the couple took turns until the hole was deep enough for burial. As they dropped the body into the ground, both began to tear up and Jonah struggled to keep his composure and be strong. He had never dealt with death in this fashion and the gravity of the situation hit him. His sad and morbid thoughts turned to concern for Dotsie. She moved from the gravesite and knelt on the ground as she cried more.

Jonah threw the last of the dirt from his shovel and it hit the grave with a finality. He dropped the shovel and wiped the perspiration from his face with his sleeve. Dotsie moved to him quietly and picked up the shovel with one hand while holding Jonah's hand with the other. The deed was complete.

Chapter Six

"They're furious...all of them. I heard my dad talking about it. A posse will be gathering tomorrow to search for you...to hunt you down and kill you. Hunter has disappeared and they think that you must have killed him. There is a meeting tonight at the old township hall and they will all be there. This is not good."

Dotsie paused and looked at Jonah, trying to gauge his expression. The young man showed a bit of concern but knew that he had to keep calm and keep his sense of reasoning sharp. He didn't want to cause Dotsie to panic. Now he had to review the plan in his mind and the worst scenario seemed to be upon him.

"It's time for me to run for it. I can't have you follow me. I have to get out or die trying... on my own."

Dotsie's face gave away a look of shock and despair; this was the last thing she had wanted. They would escape together, not apart.

"I'm going with you." she declared with bold authority.

"No, you're not." he retorted with an air of defiance.

"YES I AM!" she exclaimed with a furious look.

"You can't go with me. If they catch me they will kill me. I don't want you to die with me. I'm going alone. They will never suspect that you were helping me."

"You're forgetting one thing." she stated quietly.

"I killed Hunter."

"I don't care. You are not taking the blame for Hunter. You were protecting me, plain and simple. I was the reason you shot him and I will take the blame."

Dotsie turned away from Jonah for a moment and as she looked back a tear ran down her cheek. She spun toward him and raised her arms out in defiance, not willing to give him up.

"You can't run for the county line. They will have people looking for you and this is a bigger network of crazies than you can imagine. Hunter hasn't shown up in town and everyone is starting to panic, it's already been a week. The rumors are out that he has failed and now everyone is looking for him as well as you."

Jonah sat back against the worn wood of the old loft and silently pondered his predicament. Dotsie's mind had been a mess after she put a bullet in Hunter and having to drop Hunter into a shallow grave just made the whole situation more morbid. Jonah now wondered if he could trust her judgement.

"It seems to me that from what you said everybody is looking for me to run for the county line. Do you think they will have the state police pursuing me?"

Dotsie now sat down quietly next to Jonah as she worked her way through the puzzle.

"No. The state police don't know anything about the tradition of manhood training and the townspeople don't want that to change. Everything about it is illegal and if someone outside finds out there will be hell to pay. The whole reason this barbaric thing exists is because no one else knows about it. People don't get away...they die."

"You mean to tell me that no one has ever gotten away?" Jonah questioned with amazement.

"To the best of my knowledge...no one has ever gotten away. Some people have failed to kill their target but the townies end up killing for them. Then they get a second chance, and the second chance never fails. I don't ever remember anyone doing what you did...its usually the shooter chickening out. The few that have made a run for it have not gotten out of the park...they just kind of freak out."

The young man shook his head in a daze of unbelieving shock.

I am the first to get away? That can't be.

He lifted his head after a minute and saw the slyest of smiles cross Dotsie's face. This brought a smile to his expression.

"Ok, what gives? What is that pretty little mind of yours cooking up?"

"We are not alone." she quietly whispered.

Jonah's mindset instantly pivoted to one of fright and curiosity.

"What do you mean by we are not alone?" he whispered as he looked around the barn loft.

"Not here...we are not alone in regard to the townies. I can get some of my friends to help us. As long as you stay hidden we can work out a plan to get you...both of us...out of here."

He liked the sound of 'both of us'. His heart was quickly falling for this girl and now it sounded like she felt the same way.

"Can we trust people? All it takes is one person to turn on us and it's all over."

Dotsie paused and then reassured him.

"We can trust my friends. We have been against this ghastly practice for a long time. We just have not had a way to get rid of it. You might be the answer."

Jonah now shook his head back and forth slowly.

"I don't know, Dotsie. You're telling me a small group of your high school friends are going to fix this mess and stop a whole town from all of this?"

The pretty young teen flashed a confident smile.

"Leave it to me. We will find a way to get out of this."

****

The next morning as the sun was appearing on the horizon a group of seven classmates slowly ascended the slight hill to the old barn. Jonah had been up for a while and now felt a mix of curiosity and fear. He hid aside the open front door of the loft and peeked out at the group of friends.

As they slowly approached, Jonah realized that they were moving covertly, trying to remain undetected while their pretty leader directed them. Dotsie was moving at the front, checking both left and right for any possible detection. After assurance that the coast was clear, the crew entered the barn and one by one made it into the loft.

Introductions were made and Jonah knew it would be a while before he could attach the names to their faces. There were only six of them aside from Dotsie, but Jonah always struggled with keeping people's names straight. A smallish, pushy kid took a posture of leadership and Jonah didn't know if he could like him.

"Like Dotsie said, I'm Albert. We think its time to put the manhood test to rest for once and for all. We can help you too."

His tone of voice sounded rough, not very encouraging... as if almost rehearsed or scripted. Jonah perused the new faces surrounding him and everyone seemed to be as confident as Albert. Dotsie stepped up to quell the doubt that was now apparent on Jonah's face.

"Don't mind Al...he just sounds menacing. He's really a teddy bear."

The wannabe leader's shoulders slumped down and he shot the beauty a look of distain and pain. His ego was deflated, his feelings obviously crushed.

"I'm sorry, Albert." she said in a consoling voice as she gave him a friendly hug. Jonah watched carefully as he hoped that Dotsie and the new kid were only friends and nothing more.

The group spent the morning in the loft, going over every possible scenario and by noon they thought they had something of substance figured out. The final plan had possibilities but could also signal the death of all of them. The young rebels seemed up to the task despite the risk involved.

As everyone descended the ladder from the loft, Jonah pulled Dotsie aside quietly.

"Are you sure we can trust them? Are you sure?"

His whisper had the desperate tone of fearful emphasis as the realization that his life was now possibly further at stake.

"Trust me, Jonah. We can trust all of them."

With her quiet reassurance she gave him a quick kiss on the lips. Now his heart and mind raced in a good way and a wide smile crossed his face. She smiled back. Jonah's mind was calmed as he realized that he and Dotsie were on their way to great possibilities.

Chapter Seven

Jonah felt the fatigue of the last stressful days and he leaned his back against the old wall of the barn, falling into a deep sleep almost instantly. His mind drifted into a dream, a replay of the evening before he arrived in the small town.

There were three of them, dirty and dangerous as could be. The long knife scared him the most, its blade gleaming in the moonlight as the men approached. He had nothing to give the robbers and he realized in an instant that he could either make a run for it or die. Making his choice, he fled as fast as his legs could carry him.

A long freighter rolled down the tracks, slowly picking up momentum on his left and he veered in that direction. The threatening trio behind him could not keep up with his pace for he was much younger and more athletic. Fear propelled him to move his legs even faster and with a quick leap he rolled up and into the open freight car. Seeing the pursuers slow up, he was thankful that he didn't have to fight for his life.

Jonah collapsed against the back wall of the car, his chest heaving in a struggle to take in air as he surveyed his situation. There was one other person aboard and he was fast asleep. Finally catching his breath, Jonah looked out at the dark countryside passing in a blur and he felt a sudden twinge of homesickness overtake his thoughts. His manly pride would only allow himself one tear of pity and he wiped it away quickly, hoping the sleeper across from him didn't notice.

Not even a half hour had passed when a decrepit hobo climbed into the car at a stop in the middle of nowhere. As they began rolling onward the graybeard approached with a menacing stare.

"Gimme your money, kid." the old man commanded with a deep growl.

Jonah didn't say a word. Facing danger twice in one night, the holdup didn't even seem real to him. He stood up to face his attacker. The thief grabbed Jonah by the shoulders and shook him violently in an effort to beat the money out of his victim. Jonah wondered if the coins in his pocket were worth the battle. The money was something that he could not afford to give up.

"Leave me alone, old man!" he shouted, hoping that the sleeper would hear the commotion and come to his aid. The man slumped toward the floor, unaware of the commotion. The thief shook him harder and in a defensive move Jonah kicked his leg forward with all his might. He caught the man square in the groin and the robber let out a howl as he fell to his knees.

"You little bastard, you're going to get it now!"

Moving quickly in a freight car that is rolling along at fifty miles an hour was physically challenging, but Jonah made his move for the open side door. The ground was a blur below as he considered jumping off; survival would not be possible without major injury. He turned as the old man lunged toward him and they crashed into each other.

The train veered to the left as it headed into a bend and the car lurched suddenly with the two men caught in a violent dance. Jonah threw all his weight into the thief and then swung him through the door. The man screamed as he fell, clutching at the edge of the car for dear life. Using all the force he could muster, Jonah stomped his foot down as hard as he could and felt a crunch come from the grasping hand. With a look of sudden alarm and defeat, the old man let out one last cry as he fell under the train and out of sight.

Shaking with an adrenaline rush, Jonah dropped to the floor and vomited. After a moment, he wiped his mouth with the back of his hand and looked across the freight car. His eyes met the gaze of the now awakened onlooker. Jonah had just committed manslaughter and the man sitting upright was now a witness to the crime.

"Don't worry kid." the awakened man mumbled in a gravelly voice. "I won't say a thing. He robbed people all the time. Looks like his stealing days are over."

His heart beating out of control, Jonah slumped back against the wall of the car and let out a loud sigh.

Good lord, can things get any worse?

Chapter Eight

"NO, NO, NO, HELP ME!"

The words echoed off the wooden walls of the loft and Dotsie sat upright in an instant, her mind clouded with confusion and fear. Jonah was calling out in his sleep and she rolled over to wake him from his unconscious terror.

"Wake up, Jonah. It's alright...you're safe!"

The young man's eyes opened with fright as he tried to place his surroundings. His fears subsided suddenly when he saw Dotsie's face and he rolled into her embrace, trembling slightly.

"What's wrong?" Dotsie asked gently as she held him tightly.

It took Jonah a moment to compose himself.

"When did you get here?"

Their eyes met and her smile calmed his racing heart and mind.

"I came back and you were sleeping so soundly that I didn't want to wake you. I just cuddled up against you. Are you better now?"

Jonah hugged her tightly for a minute, lost in her wonderful embrace. The world was perfect in her arms and he began to explain himself to keep her from worrying.

"I was dreaming, I think. I was dreaming about the train."

"What train, Jonah?"

He was almost embarrassed to confide in his new love interest, fearing it would make him look weak.

"You can tell me, Jonah. You can always trust me."

He looked into her eyes and relayed the dream in its entirety, including the part about pushing the robber out of the door and out of his life.

While Dotsie trusted her safety with Jonah, she also was surprised that he could kill a man so suddenly. Then it occurred to her that anyone could kill in self-defense and she was a prime example herself.

"You're alright now, Jonah, and that's what counts. I will always protect you...whatever happens."

He moved to her and kissed her softly on her lips. Then he whispered softly to her.

"We are both killers."

The couple stared at each another with a quiet, somber realization. Confusion, panic, sadness, and teen love clouded their minds in a strange twist of emotions. Neither could think of a word to share. Then the barn door opened below the loft and their attention shifted to curiosity and fear.

The young lovers gathered themselves quickly and moved to the back of the loft to hide. Albert's creepy face appeared over the top of the ladder with the rest of the friendly crew in tow.

"The meeting is tonight...we are ready for them." he declared with authority.

The last of the group was now standing in the loft and all of them had looks of evil determination. Jonah feared the plan they had in mind; it couldn't be good. Dotsie moved into the circle of rebellion and Jonah now realized that he was standing alone, outside of the group.

"We have an idea and it does not involve you. You don't need to know about any of it. Just lay low in here and before you know it you will be free."

Jonah looked to Dotsie for information or reassurance and she just smiled in the same crazed manner that the rest of the group did. The look made the hairs on Jonah's arms stand at attention; the look was one that conveyed evil of an inhumane nature. He wasn't going to press his luck and pursue answers to his questions and so he turned away for a moment and tried to calm his mind.

When Jonah turned back toward the classmates he quickly realized that the rest of the group had moved out of the loft and were on their way out of the building. Only Dotsie remained and she appeared to be back to her old self with a tender smile. She moved silently to embrace him and he held her with emotion. She felt perfect in his arms.

Jonah could no longer resist the urge and a long and passionate kiss followed. Dotsie melted into his arms and Jonah's mind was enveloped in love. He had never felt this way about anyone before and judging from her reaction, Dotsie had not experienced it either.

Time seemed to stand still and a quarter of an hour later they self-consciously regained their composure. Then the questions in Jonah's mind began to flow.

"Dotsie, please tell me what is going on. What are you going to do?"

Jonah's voice was soft but had an air of pleading within it.

"I can't tell you. I'm not so sure myself. The group has a plan. According to them there are plenty of people in town who would like to see the manhood test abolished...done away with forever. The group knows what they are doing...I am going to trust them and I think you should too."

She scurried down the ladder and was gone before Jonah could pry more answers from her. He counted on the most important thing...he knew that Dotsie would come back to him and he would count the minutes until she returned.

****

The old township hall had been around since the Civil War, in fact some of the local historians dated it back to the first encounters between the Europeans and the Dakota Sioux, the indigenous tribes. Regardless of the building's actual age, it showed signs of dilapidation and most were certain that its demise was near.

The building had a certain historical charm on the inside however, and the town leaders had a special affinity for the gathering place. It wasn't designed for space, it held less than twenty-five people comfortably, and on this warm night about twenty-five citizens would be all it would accommodate comfortably.

The gatherers were the chosen nobility in the town; the men were the richest and most powerful of the small community. They all had one thing in common and that was their hold on the precious status they had achieved.

The manhood training that they cherished had been passed down from a time when it was easy to dispose of the unwanted, in particular the wanderers and some Native Americans that wandered throughout the area.

Making it a ritual seemed to make it moral in the eyes of the townspeople and nothing attracts a crowd like death. The execution achieved some important goals as it built up the righteousness, the dominance, and the manliness of the townspeople and it got rid of those that were not desired.

Times had changed but the ritual had not. While it was less frequent it was still a big event, especially for the town elders and their families. Status was affirmed with every execution and now the leaders would not let one manhood training gone bad stand in the way of their cherished right.

This time things were different, and not in a good way. An emergency meeting was called for the most prominent leaders, a group that included both Hunter's and Dotsie's fathers and grandfathers. It was tradition to wait until sundown to gather as the late evening would provide cool air in the small, closed structure.

This meeting had added significance. Hunter Carlyle had not returned from his quest. The popular young man had simply disappeared into thin air and now his family and friends were in distress. They feared the worst and hoped for a better answer than what the predicted reality would provide.

The men would come up with the answers and as the past had proven everything would work out in the end. The elders filed into the tiny wooden structure with great dignity, enveloped in self-importance. A small, glassless window opening on each side of the room was closed shut by the men to keep confidentiality. The air inside would become stifling and so they moved quickly to the pressing business at hand.

"Come on, Dennis, we gotta move quick!"

Albert ran slightly ahead of his younger but larger friend, a young man who many of the townspeople regarded as slow of mind. The big teen stopped suddenly, causing his leader to halt.

"We shouldn't do this Al."

"Don't be a weakling, Dennis. Follow me and for god's sake stay quiet."

The compliant friend was used to taking orders from Albert and he continued to move at a slow but steady pace toward the building.

Dusk had cast an eerie shadow across the central expanse and the town square seemed deserted. Both boys looked around them and saw no one. The faint sound of a popular radio show drifted from the open windows of the neighboring homes into the warm night. Muffled dialogue was followed by family laughter, chatter, and profound enjoyment. The realization that everyone was be gathered in their living rooms to enjoy this entertainment gave Albert a sense of security as he grinned in anticipation of carrying out his plan.

An iron bar three feet long slid quietly into the handles of the front door. The closed shutters were locked the same way. The men in the building had no idea of what was happening outside.

The impromptu meeting was called to order by the sheriff and the men found a space to settle in their crowded confines.

"We all know why we are here. Hunter Carlyle remains missing and it is pretty apparent that the visitor is involved in his disappearance. I'm not going to commit to the idea that Hunter is dead, instead I think the kid is still hunting. He needs our help."

The men turned to judge the effect of the statement on Hunter's father and he nodded with hope that his son was fine. The sheriff continued.

"There's only two ways to get out of this town, either by the main road or by rail. My department has both well-covered and we can rely on neighboring counties for their help. I have already put out a bulletin that states that the young man is wanted for burglary. This shouldn't raise too much suspicion, the kid will be caught and transported to us. Our visitor will not get far before he is caught, I can assure you of that."

A faint smell of petrol permeated the walls of the structure and the men began to exhibit puzzled looks as the odor intensified. The realization of what was happening took place too late. Black smoke started rolling in from the floor and walls as their puzzlement turned to panic.

A rush for the front door proved fruitless as the iron bar held the double doors in place. Turning to the shuttered windows on each side of the structure, the men made a dash to them and pushed hard to get them to open. The bars held firm. Now the flames were piercing the floor and walls and one by one the men began passing out from the smoke.

By the time the fire department arrived there was little left of the structure; the wooden building went up like a tinder box.

Realization that there had been men inside, including their beloved Fire Chief and respected Sheriff, brought visible grief from the people whose task it was to save the building and the lives of those inside.

A proud spectator stood across the street and when the opportunity arose, explained to the person next to them that the firemen thought the archaic electrical wiring had malfunctioned. It was an unfortunate accident indeed. The informed observer couldn't, however, contain a tiny smile derived from a job well done.

Chapter Nine

The group of rebels fought through the darkness as they made their way back to the hiding place. Their covert arrival was a surprise to Jonah and Dotsie, who were enjoying some private time and romance.

"Did you hear what happened in town? It's unbelievable! The old township hall burned to the ground...completely gone. The meeting to catch you went up in smoke!"

Dotsie turned to Jonah in horror as the realization of what happened hit her. Then her attention went back to Albert.

"Was there a meeting of the elders? Was my dad there? My grandpa?" She trembled with the questions, fearful of the answer that Albert would provide.

"I don't know. All I know is the township hall is completely gone...it's all ashes."

Silence fell across the loft as everyone avoided further questions. Then Dotsie stood up and headed for the ladder quickly.

"I must find out what happened. I will be back in the morning."

Her statement was directed toward Jonah and he moved to the ladder and held her in a quick, final embrace. She shimmied down the ladder and was gone in a flash. The rest of the group fled behind her, leaving Jonah alone with questions of his own.

The next morning the devastating fire was the talk of the town and, as all gossip flows, the cause was quickly determined by the townspeople to be the decrepit, faulty electrical wiring. Blame was passed around concerning who was responsible for the structure and its upkeep; no one was the wiser to the real cause of the tragedy.

Albert Crenshaw stood across the street from the smoldering pile of ruins and stared as if in a trance. People were still walking by and stopping to inspect the carnage and it was now determined that all of the most important elders had perished. Members of their families stood aside with tears and occasional wailing as remnants of bodies were retrieved.

No one could be identified, but Dotsie stood silently in the crowd and reality set in; she knew that her father and grandfather were gone. She was cold inside, unsure how to feel. As she looked around, she couldn't help but feel that she should have been crying as well but the tears would not come.

Instead of becoming overwhelmed with grief like the rest of the crowd, a sense of calming relief passed through her mind.

"I will never be used again...my nightmare is over." Dotsie whispered to herself.

A look that should have conveyed sadness was overtaken by a glaring one of fierce determination. The young lady stared at the smoldering ruins and then slowly surveyed the crowd around her as they displayed a quiet shock and sorrow.

If they only knew.

The trouble started shortly after her mother passed away. Dotsie was twelve years old and was just beginning to blossom into a young woman. She had a bright future in front of her and she excelled at almost everything she pursued in life. Attention was now being focused on her, both from the townspeople who felt sorry for her and from the men of the town who could not help but notice her innocent beauty.

Her innocence was taken by the very men she trusted, her father and grandfather, and a downward spiral began in her life. To her credit, Dotsie survived as best as she could, but she would be scarred for life. The flaming demise of her tormentors brought a new life and peace of mind that she had wanted for so long.

I hope it hurt...I hope they burn in hell.

Walking with her head down through the maze of mourners and spectators, she quietly accepted condolences from those who knew her. Turning the corner of the block of retail stores on the main street, she moved away from all with a satisfied grin on her face.

Within an hour she was back at the barn with the only person who she felt she could really trust, the only person who really loved her. As she took each step closer, she admired the wild daisies that grew in the sun-blessed field. By the time she reached the large double doors of the structure her demeanor had become as bright as the flowery expanse.

She climbed the ladder carefully and found Jonah sleeping in a far corner on a bunch of blankets that she had brought him earlier. He had no idea she was there and she quietly sat down in the middle of the loft and admired him as he slept. Jonah slowly woke to see his love gazing at him.

"Hey. You look beautiful." He purred with a smile.

"You're the one that is beautiful." Dotsie replied with a new spark of life that shone through.

"So, tell me what happened? You seem really happy, the news must be good."

The young lady nodded with a smile.

"It's very good. They are both dead."

Confusion crossed Jonah's mind and his expression conveyed one of puzzlement.

"What do you mean they? Who's dead?"

"My dad and my grandfather. They are dead. I shouldn't even call them dad and grandfather. They don't deserve it. Now they are gone, thank God."

A quiet and strange laugh now seemingly possessed Dotsie and it scared him.

"What the hell are you talking about? Why are you happy?"

The smile left her face.

"You don't want to know. Anyhow, this will change the town...all the elders are dead. Now maybe we will be safe and just maybe the manhood ritual will finally be gone. The big question is who will take over the town. I think it's time for a youthful revolution."

The couple stood up together and Jonah moved to her calmly and pulled her into a comforting embrace.

"I'm confused as hell, but I am sure happy you are here. I missed you."

Dotsie's demeanor softened as she hugged her boyfriend harder.

"I missed you too. Now we have to get you out of here safely. Get both of us out of here safely."

Jonah smiled as a comforting warmth enveloped him.

She said both of us.

Chapter Ten

As with so many things in life the suddenness of tragedy can drown out the front-page news of the day before, but the most important events seem to slowly make their way back into consciousness. This was no different.

Thomas Jefferson Johnson was the next in line for Sheriff. His predecessor had gone up in flames the evening before, and there was really no one else qualified to take the lead job. Whether he wanted it or not, he was the next man up.

The young deputy was not a native of the community, in fact he had traveled to the region from more northern reaches and he was still somewhat new to the town, its people, and the difference in culture from what he was raised in.

At the ripe young age of twenty-one, Thomas Johnson didn't feel deserving much less able to hold the highest law enforcement position in the county. He had only been on the force for a year. He didn't even serve as an officer in this small town for he had started his law enforcement career in a neighboring village that no one seemed to notice or care about. His biggest cases focused on providing the town drunkard a place to sleep off his daily habit and rescuing cats from trees. This sudden rise in position and stature was certainly unexpected and not entirely welcome.

To make matters more difficult he realized that he was now responsible for solving the greatest mystery to ever hit this locale, at least as far back as anyone could remember. This situation could make or break his career and his reputation.

The biggest problem was that he didn't even know where to start. This realization hit him like a lightning bolt as he entered the city jail, a small single-story brick building down the block from the ashes of the township hall.

Good Lord, here we go...please help me.

"Good morning, Tom. Welcome to our beautiful little community. My name is Helen Anderson, I will be your assistant."

The official county secretary was seated at the main desk in what was considered the lobby but was in reality just a larger room than the rest of the rooms in the building. A worn oak counter sat on an elevated wooden platform designed to protect her from the criminal element that might want to cause her harm.

"I am pleased to meet you, Helen." he replied with a sheepishness that only a hesitant rookie could demonstrate.

"Are you ready to start your new job?" the friendly, middle-aged clerk asked. Her compassionate, motherly demeanor put the young lawman at ease.

"I guess I don't have a choice...with the boss gone and all."

Both bowed their heads unconsciously with the realization that the old boss was no longer there.

The young officer had to mentally and physically force himself to occupy the office of his superior. He had only met the previous sheriff on a couple of formal occasions, but he also knew that the old man had watched over him from a distance and had offered support if needed. The sheriff's office space seemed somewhat creepy in a ghostly way and he felt out of place inside it. He moved with a quiet reverence to his new desk and pondered his next move, the next chapter in his life.

"What the hell am I going to do? I barely know my job as a deputy...now I have to run the place?" he murmured to himself while wallowing in a moment of self-pity.

At least I wasn't at that meeting last night.

One could say he was legitimately in the dark concerning much of the job. The day before he was a newbie in the neighboring county and now he was a suddenly appointed leader in what felt like a strange land. He had heard rumors about weird events that took place in his new locale but chose not to believe them. Johnson had operated for as long as he could remember on the idea that ignorance could be bliss; too much knowledge could cause sleepless nights.

Don't get yourself involved in things you don't understand.   You will learn about everything in due time.

Helen would have to fill him in on how the daily schedule worked. It was a solid bet that she was the most informed person in the town, maybe even the county. She could be his greatest asset, his source for all his needs. Thomas hoped she would tutor him because in his mind she was the actual one running the office and county.

The knowledgeable desk clerk approached her new boss and sat down across the desk. Although she had a deep loyalty and respect for her former boss, Helen found the old sheriff difficult to work with and relate to. She hoped her relationship with Tom would be easier to live with.

"Well, I suppose we should do some work here, right?" she offered with a quiet chuckle in an effort to break the ice.

"Yes, but I really don't know what the hell to do." the rookie said with arms out and palms to the ceiling.

"Do you know anything about the Hunter Carlyle case here in town? He went missing a few weeks ago and most of the townspeople think he was killed by a young wanderer. A young man who just showed up one day. Folks around here are calling him the devil kid."

The new sheriff's jaw dropped slightly and his eyes narrowed as if he didn't know whether to believe Helen or not.

"The Devil Kid?"

His assistant locked eyes with him and nodded in the affirmative.

"Sheriff Ramsey was working on finding this kid that is now on the run. He suspected that Hunter was either with the kid or killed by him. Ramsey didn't tell me much...he kept most of the business to himself. I guess a good place to start would be to try and find Hunter and the runaway kid."

"The Devil Kid." the young man repeated quietly to himself.

"Uh huh. Strange name, right?"

Johnson sat quietly as he wondered whether he could really trust Helen and her information. Was this some kind of joke to spring on the rookie sheriff? He had to put his trust in his assistant, there was no other choice.

"So, can you tell me why the kid was on the run and why Hunter of all people would have been pursuing him?"

The clerk leaned in and placed her elbows on the desk while brandishing a grin.

"Oh, you don't know? You are not going to believe this..."

****

Despite a blinding sun and unbearable late afternoon heat, Thomas Johnson stood near the charred remains from the events of the evening before. The building was leveled and charred pitch black with whisps of smoke drifting upward from the pile. An aroma hung in the air and it took a moment for the new sheriff to identify its source.

"Burnt human flesh." He whispered to himself as he trembled lightly for a moment with revulsion.

"You never really get used to it. Right?"

The man had moved up from behind him and had startled him.

"I'm Paul Redding. The new fire chief as of this morning. A godawful shame, huh? I take it you're Sheriff Johnson?"

Thomas nodded quietly, not quite knowing what to say. He took a moment to look over the slightly older professional, who had the build of a brick wall and yet had a surprisingly soft and friendly disposition. Redding held out his hand and a firm handshake sealed their introduction.

"This is a hell of a way to get a promotion, right?"

Sheriff Johnson returned a smile with a nod and felt a brotherly connection with Redding almost instantly.

"You can say that again. I'm not even from here...I got summoned this morning before sunrise. Yesterday I was a deputy over in Pierce County, today I'm the new boss."

Both men shook their heads in disbelief as they turned their attention to the smoldering pile of death.

"Damn, there's really nothing left. Was it intentional?" the sheriff asked in his best professional tone.

"Hard to say. There is a good possibility that an accelerant was used, probably petrol. The structure must've really went up quick. By the time we arrived there was nothing left, no hope for survivors. I'm guessing most were dead from smoke before the flames got them. There is a possibility that it could have been some sort of an electrical malfunction, but it wouldn't have burned so quick."

Johnson kept quiet with the realization that he was talking to someone with much more experience when it came to fire. He moved forward as his eyes caught hold of an object.

"This is strange though. Look at this iron bar. I can't seem to place it or what it does. What do you think, Paul?"

The trained firefighter looked at the strange piece of darkened, bent iron and kicked it with his boot. He slowly made his way around the scene and pointed to another while deep in thought. Johnson followed and both turned suddenly to face each other with a knowing expression. The fire chief was the first to vent the realization out loud.

"Damn, they were trapped in there when it went up."

The words hung in the air for what seemed like an eternity. The sheriff looked around the square carefully, noting the buildings and their proximity to the crime scene. His new office was down the street to his left and across the street was a row of houses.

"Looks like a possible multiple homicide case. Chief, if you don't mind, I'm going to take a walk down here and maybe talk to some people to find out if anyone saw anything. A little detective work, right? It was nice to meet you, I'm sure we will be spending a lot of time on this one, huh?"

"It was nice to meet you too, Sheriff. I think you are right about this one, it's definitely a homicide crime scene. Good luck with your detective work."

Thomas Jefferson Johnson went to work.

Chapter Eleven

"I heard from a couple of the boys over at Murphy's drug store that the escapee did it...he killed Hunter and then set the hall on fire. He's going to kill all of us as revenge for what we did."

Dotsie stepped back, visibly stunned by the news from the elderly busybody who was well known for her ability to gossip.

"What do you mean by escapee? They haven't caught him yet? Do they have any idea where he is?"

Mrs. Rose leaned in, her seemingly frail body invading the girl's space. She lowered her voice and looked around as if she was giving valuable, secret information.

"The kid that ran away, the one Hunter was supposed to...you know. He's at large and he killed Hunter and set the fire. No one knows where he is."

"Who told you all of this?"

The gossiper smiled and hushed her tone further, enjoying the attention she was getting.

"Some of the young men down at the store. Dennis Reed and that little Albert kid. The little guy sure likes attention. He was talking up a storm for the whole world to hear. He says the killer is the Devil Kid."

Dotsie's jaw dropped at the mention of Albert. There was only one Albert that was small in stature but big on talk.

"The Devil Kid?" Dotsie repeated with shock.

"That's what that Albert kid called him. I think it's ridiculous personally."

"I'm sorry Mrs. Rose, but I have to run...a lot to do you know."

"My poor dear, I'm so sorry for what you are going through. If you need anything, please feel free to ask. I am here to help, you poor dear girl."

With that last offer the elderly lady stepped forward and gave Dotsie an aggressive hug. The young woman felt smothered by the overly friendly move and gently pushed away apologetically.

"I must go. I just remembered something very important. It's nice to see you, Mrs. Rose."

Dotsie struggled to keep her balance as she sprinted to the front of the store with a full basket of groceries. She paid quickly, waited impatiently for the young carryout boy to bag her food up, and then hurried to the barn outside of town.

"Pack up your stuff, we have to go NOW!" she yelled as she entered the building and approached the loft.

"What do you mean by WE HAVE TO GO NOW?" Jonah retorted with fear.

"Just do what I say, I'll tell you all about it later. Get your stuff, we must hurry!"

Jonah grabbed his blankets and rolled them up as best he could. Within a minute the couple headed for the woods at a fast pace while scouting for danger.

"Dotsie, where are we going?"

Both were out of breath and took a moment to recover while staying cautious. The dark coolness of the canopy of trees gave them a false sense of comfort and security.

"We are going to my house. There is no longer anyone there, it's a safe place for you to hide until we figure this thing out."

"YOUR HOUSE? Are you kidding? There are people there."

"Not anymore. Everybody is dead but me. It's creepy, I know, but safe for now."

Jonah looked at her suspiciously as he tried to sort the situation out in his mind.

If I can't trust her, who can I trust? I don't have a choice.

"Why the hurry? What is going on?"

Dotsie began to walk again at a fast pace.

"Mrs. Rose, the town gossip, overheard Albert saying that you killed Hunter and all the men at the meeting."

Jonah rolled his eyes while following his lover.

"That's just gossip. No one will really believe that, will they?"

Dotsie turned to Jonah suddenly and shot him a look of condescending disbelief, almost offensive in nature.

"Believe it? Are you kidding? Of course they will believe it! You are already the bad guy; it will be easy to pin the blame for all of this on you. Their cozy little town was perfect until you came along. The person that catches you will be a hero in this town for the rest of their life. Albert is spreading the lies...he is behind all of this. He has already given you a nickname. The Devil Kid."

"The Devil Kid?"

Jonah let out a disbelieving chuckle and then continued his questioning.

"What makes you believe Albert is behind this? How do you know what you heard is true? He's on our side, right?"

"That's what you think, that is what HE wants you to think. He was overheard spreading the lies and I have no doubt that somehow he was involved in starting the fire at the hall. That's Albert for you."

An uneasy silence fell over them as they continued through the woods, finally reaching the meadow where Jonah saw Dotsie for the first time. The couple visually scanned the surrounding area and, seeing no danger, quickly made their way across the sunny expanse and onto the homestead property.

Opening the back door, an uneasy silence permeated the kitchen and Dotsie set the satchel of groceries down and began to cry.

"I'm alone in this world, my family is gone."

Jonah put his arms around her as she trembled and sobbed into his shoulder.

"You're not alone. You have me."

****

Albert Crenshaw sat quietly in the shade at a picnic table in the local park. He watched the stream roll by and listened intently as the water created a soothing music for his mind. The day was going to be a hot one and so a cool, quiet refuge such as this was a welcome necessity.

He began talking to himself in a very low, quiet tone. Working out the next phase of his plan was essential and he was actually pleasantly surprised at how successful his planned arson was. No one was the wiser as to what really happened.

"The fire was good. It felt so good to see all those asses burning. Now it's my turn to rule."

He repeated his last sentence three more times to solidify his plan in his mind.

"Tonight I will go to the barn and capture the devil kid. I'll be a hero! I need to find a gun..."

Albert's voice trailed off as he looked all around him for possible snoops. He relaxed when he realized that he was alone and he continued to plot.

"Dotsie's going to be a problem...she's in love with him. What does he have that I don't have? I'm smarter, better looking, a better guy than him. Where the hell did he come from anyway? I will shoot him if I must. Maybe shoot Dotsie too? I really hope I don't have to...she will love me after I become a hero. She will love me...she will love me..."

He stopped muttering to himself and sat in silence, mentally hypnotized by the sound and sight of the bubbling stream. Time seemed to stand still as he watched the rivulets of water cascade upon one another, suddenly there and then suddenly submerged and gone.

"I need a gun. Dotsie's dad has guns...had guns, ha, ha, ha."

Chapter Twelve

"Someone's pounding on the door...they're knocking."

Jonah was suddenly awakened and his mind was reeling from the quick roust. It took a moment for him to realize where he was and then he rolled over to face Dotsie. He gently shook her arm and she rolled over to face him.

"Dots...someone is downstairs!"

The young woman shot up in bed as if she was hit with a lightning bolt and her expression of fear shook Jonah to his core.

"What are we going to do? Who could it be?" Jonah asked, not realizing that he knew almost no one and that her answer would probably be meaningless.

"How should I know?" Dotsie answered in a near hysteric state while she moved out of the room and down the stairs toward the pounding.

As she reached the bottom landing, Dotsie slowly peeked around the corner and tried to recognize the person at the front door. The decorative lace curtains hung across a small window that partially hid his face, but she could tell that it was Albert Crenshaw standing on the front steps.

Quietly sneaking back up the stairs, the look of surprise and disbelief gave Jonah reason to be fearful.

"Dotsie, who is it... Who's downstairs?" he questioned with quiet urgency.

"You're not going to believe it...it's Albert!"

"Albert? What does he want here?"

"How should I know?" Dotsie answered with a wild gesture, as freaked out as Jonah was.

"How should we get rid of him?"

Dotsie prayed that the front door was secure, or things could get crazy in a hurry. Both could hear Albert trying to enter, deterred by the lock.

"He can't see us if we stay up here. He'll go away sooner or later." she stated with assurance.

"Hopefully sooner!" Jonah suddenly giggled as he pulled Dotsie down on the bed.

"Hey! This is serious! If he finds us we could be in BIG trouble."

After a minute or two, Dotsie slowly pulled a curtain aside and peaked out of her bedroom window to see Albert making his way across the bright meadow. He was headed for the old barn far away.

The teens laid low and stayed hidden from the world. As time started to tick again both began to feel a domestic peace that brought them closer every day.

I could spend the rest of my life with this girl.

The smile that occupied his face was so bright that it caught Dotsie's attention immediately.

"What are you grinning about?" she asked as she returned the smile with a pretty one of her own.

"Oh, nothing. Just us."

****

The meeting in the old barn seemed incomplete without Dotsie. She had always been present because she had created the teen crew and she was the self-appointed leader. Albert was happy that she wasn't there because he could run the show on his own, but his heart also missed her.

"As you know, Dotsie is missing and I'm guessing she is with that guy."

Albert hesitated, frowned in a menacing way, and then purposely omitted Jonah's name in an effort to downgrade him.

"Margie, do you know where Dotsie is?"

Margaret Reed was questioned first as she was Dotsie's best friend.

"I have no idea where she is. I stopped by her house yesterday and no one answered. I'm really worried about her."

The concern was genuine and Margie told herself she would have to check on her friend again. The questions from Albert continued and soon the group understood the urgency of finding Dotsie and establishing support from their community. They also understood that Albert seemed to have an underlying motive, and when the meeting finally broke up, there was a new reason to be scared.

Margie walked from the old barn back to town and then veered off on a side street to double back from where she came. A half hour later, with darkness descended on the community, she found herself standing on Dotsie's front steps. She knocked quietly, hoping not to attract outside attention but just loud enough to be heard inside.

"It's Margie. We can trust her." Dotsie whispered to Jonah while checking the front porch. She cautiously pulled the front door toward her.

"Dotsie, my god, we've been worried about you!" her friend exclaimed as she moved forward with an urgent hug.

"Take it easy, Margie, you're going to kill me!" Dotsie giggled, pleased to see her best friend.

"How come you weren't at the meeting? You haven't answered the phone or your door. Where have you been? Have you been with Jonah? Where is he now?"

The questions flew so quickly that Dotsie could hardly keep up. She just smiled as she let her friend ramble on. Finally, as Margie ran out of breath, there was a pause.

"Well, where do I start? Let's see...I wasn't invited to any meeting, mostly because I am avoiding Albert."

Margie's face showed noticeable surprise, but she let her friend continue.

"I have not been answering the phone or the door because I am in hiding...yes, Jonah is here. He's upstairs in my room."

Margie smiled with newfound curiosity and a bit of jealousy. Her hunch proved true; Dotsie and Jonah were a couple. Jonah entered the front parlor from the kitchen with apprehension as he didn't know Margie well and wasn't sure if he could trust her. He had only seen her at the barn once or twice and she had been very reserved.

"Hi Jonah."

"Hi Margie."

An awkward amount of tension filled the air and Dotsie broke through it by sitting down on a worn sofa next to Jonah. The boyfriend and best friend seemed locked in a stare down and so the answers to the questions continued.

"Jonah has been here with me. We are hiding from the townspeople and now Albert. My dad and grandpa are now gone and so it is time for me to go. I want to leave with Jonah, but if he gets caught...if we get caught, it will be the end of us."

Margie's gaze bounced between her best friend and the hunted new kid and she was momentarily stunned and confused.

"What do you mean? He's the one in trouble, not you. You can't leave."

An unpleasant quietness took over the room that seemed to last forever. Dotsie broke the tension again.

"We are both in trouble. Jonah didn't do anything wrong and they are all trying to kill him, including Albert. I have been hiding him and so I am in trouble as well. We have to get out of the county. Jonah is going to California and I want to go with him."

Margie's heart dropped and her eyes found the floor with the realization that she was losing her best friend. Dotsie moved next to her friend and wrapped her arms around her in a soft embrace.

"I'm not going away forever, just until some things change in this town. We can stay in touch."

Margie turned to her friend with a look of surprise.

"What's going to change? What do you want to change?"

Chapter Thirteen

"Dotsie! I know you're in there. Open the door and let me in!"

The tone of Albert's voice was one of a command more than a plead and it was meant to scare the girl.

"Damn, it's Albert!" she whispered in a panic as she spun toward the top of the stairs.

"What do we do?" she asked Jonah with urgency.

"Don't answer the door." He replied calmly while looking around to survey all his options in case the visitor at the front door made his way into the house.

The doorknob rattled and the wooden barrier sounded like it was about to yield to the force that Albert was putting on it.

"Open up or I'll get the sheriff and you'll both be in trouble!"

Dotsie's eyes showed desperation as she turned back to Jonah.

"Give me a minute to get hidden, then open the door for him. He won't find me."

Jonah's calm demeanor carried over to the young lady and she nodded with belief in his idea.

"I'll be right down, Al, just give me a second to get decent!"

Her voice echoed through the empty house as Jonah grabbed his bag of belongings and crawled through the window in the back of the house. Closing the window screen behind him, he was now standing two stories up on a very slanted roof and he moved with nimbleness and caution.

Dotsie slowly descended the stairs to the entry way and parted the curtain to find an enraged Albert.

"Open the door!" he screamed with rage.

She unlocked the deadbolt and the door gave way, almost hitting her as Albert pushed his way past.

"Where is he? I know he's here."

"You mean Jonah? He's not here."

"Don't lie to me, I can tell when you are lying. Where is he?"

This brought a sudden rage to Dotsie and she snapped back at the intruder.

"Who do you think you are? How dare you come into my house and make wild accusations about me! You have no right and no reason to be here, and I should get the sheriff myself and have you arrested for trespassing!"

This made the small man back off and change his approach in the effort to locate Jonah. His voice and tone were now full of friendly concern.

"You don't have to notify anyone about me, I'm just here to protect you. He killed all those people in the fire and he killed Hunter. I'm just worried that he might come for you next."

Dotsie knew that she had control of Albert and now began to play him as a friend.

"You know you don't have to take care of me, I can take care of myself just fine. Jonah is gone, I don't know where, but he won't hurt me. He's run off scared and won't be around to hurt any of us."

"You don't mind if I take a look around for him, to protect you of course?"

"Go ahead. He is not here and I have absolutely have nothing to hide."

Albert made his way around the first floor carefully as Jonah could be around any corner and could jump out at them. With a quick visual search of each room, Albert became more frustrated. Dotsie had a condescending remark with each failed attempt.

"See, I told you he's not here. Why don't you believe me?"

After a thorough search, the young man made his way up the stairs to the second-floor landing. He suddenly turned back toward Dotsie to gauge her expression with hopes that she would give Jonah away. She was as cool as could be and stared back with an air of impatience and victory. Maybe Albert would give up.

Her heart began to race in her chest as he turned and entered her room. She said a quick silent prayer that Jonah was well hid and then waited for Albert to return.

Jonah was now perched on the roof with his back against the outside wall. He had two feet of the roof overhang to stand on and he wondered if the structure would hold his weight. The shuffling and loud movement on the other side of the wall indicated to him that Albert was intensely searching this particular room. Jonah held his breath and stayed as quiet as he could.

The pursuer returned to the landing and descended the stairs toward Dotsie.

"Well Dots, nobody there, huh?"

"I told you that you wouldn't find Jonah. Why didn't you believe me?"

A sly smile crossed his face as he slowly shook his head back and forth.

"I learned a long time ago to not believe everything I hear. One can never be too cautious, right?"

Albert's eyes turned toward the small dining table on his left and he noticed the firearm lying out in the open.

"What's this?" he questioned in a casual yet accusatory manner.

"It's my dad's. I will have to sell it...I have no use for it and don't know how to fire it."

Albert picked up the pistol and moved it from hand to hand as he inspected it. He knew little about guns but pretended to be an expert to woo Dotsie.

"Impressive. Don't you want to keep it for protection? What if Jonah comes back for you? You might need to protect yourself."

"I don't want it. I can't stand those things. You go ahead and take it... I don't want it."

Albert smiled as he took the weapon and moved toward the door. He was hoping she would invite him to stay but guessed she was in no mood for his company.

"You had better go. If the neighbors see you here with me alone they will get the wrong idea."

"Is that a bad thing? You and me, both of us together?"

His flirtatious attitude and creepy smile made her almost vomit. Albert was absolutely repulsive to her at this moment and she wished she held the pistol. A quick bullet to his head would solve the problem for once and for all.

"Al, I like you as a friend. I am not ready for anything more. Maybe someday, but not now. There's too much going on in my life. With my dad and grandfather gone, things are too complicated. I just need time."

The young man figured that he had better cut his losses and vowed to himself that he would try again. She was too beautiful to let go.

He let himself out and she watched him walk down the short lane to the dirt road. Turning in a flash she sprinted up the stairs, taking them two at a time, in hopes of finding Jonah. When she entered her room she found him sitting on her bed with a smile on his face.

"You gave him the pistol, didn't you?"

"Yep, he didn't even give it a second thought. He just took it and then he propositioned me. The nerve of him!"

"I would have propositioned you too. You would not have been able to turn me down."

His smile won her heart and she jumped on him, both tumbling onto the bed as they laughed.

Chapter Fourteen

Dotsie made her way with quiet caution across Main Street and into the local grocery store. Grabbing a hand basket, she started down the narrow aisles in search of food that would not spoil.

Making sure not to take too much and arouse suspicion, she picked items carefully and did the math in her head. The money she had from her father's top dresser drawer had to last a long time. As she turned the corner toward the meat counter she was suddenly face to face with Mrs. Rose, the local gossip.

"Dotsie, my dear! How are you? Are you alright? It's such a shame what happened."

Dotsie dropped her gaze to the floor and gave her best impression of someone in the depths of grief.

"You should let me take care of you. It's not proper for a young woman of your age to be living alone, in that house no less. You should pack some belongings and move in with me for a while, it will be good for you. Good for the both of us!"

The invitation was heartfelt and brought a genuine smile to Dotsie's face.

"I appreciate your offer, Mrs. Rose, but I think I will be fine at my house. The familiarity of my home is a good thing, it is helping me cope with the loss. It is so sweet of you to offer your home to me...I am truly blessed."

The old lady's disappointment was evident. Since her husband had passed years earlier she was lonely and the idea of a young person sharing her house gave her joy. It was not to be.

"Well dear, my invitation is open to you anytime. If you need anything, please let me know. You're such a sweet girl...you remind me a little of myself when I was young, once upon a time."

Mrs. Rose smiled and let out a light giggle as she reached out and patted Dotsie's arm. Dotsie nodded with a grin of her own. She had always liked the old lady and the reassurance of her well-being gave her a warm glow.

"Thank you so much, Mrs. Rose...you're very generous, really a saint."

Dotsie paid for her items and carried the bag of goods carefully as she couldn't afford to drop anything. Looking over her shoulder as she approached her family farmstead, she saw no one and entered the safety of her quiet abode. Jonah peeked around the corner at the top of the stairs and smiled.

"Got some good stuff. Want to see?"

"Yes, I'm starving!"

His eager smile warmed Dotsie's heart and she paused what she was doing to study him.

"What?"

Jonah noticed her and smiled back.

"Nothing."

Dotsie's smile got wider and the two had a moment of romantic connection.

"You're beautiful, you know that?"

The young woman blushed and looked down, then back at her love interest.

Groceries were laid out on the kitchen table and Jonah helped himself to a sampling as Dotsie watched him and laughed.

"Hey, don't eat it all now!" she joked with a smile that matched his.

Moments like this were priceless to her and she found herself drifting back into the bliss of being his girl.

****

The two young women cautiously made their way across the open farm field under the cover of night, a haunting hiss of a kerosine lantern guiding them slowly ahead. Each carried a spade shovel. Not a word was spoken and their labored breathing seemed loud enough to give their presence away. Margie finally broke the cold silence.

"What in the world are we doing out here? Have you lost your mind?"

Dotsie sheepishly turned away from her friend for a moment and tears began to fill her eyes.

"Someone must find him. He deserves a proper burial. He didn't mean to do all this; he was a good kid with a kind heart. Those men in town turned him into a killing animal. He didn't deserve this."

Her sobbing got louder as her shoulders shook and Margie took her in a tender embrace to sooth her and quiet her down before they got caught.

"What if someone sees us...what if we get caught?"

The crying subsided and Dotsie regained her composure.

"No one will see us. We need him to be found."

A quarter mile later they moved past the old barn and along a mature tree line that hid them even better. Dotsie spoke first in a slow, hushed whisper.

"I think he's right about here. Between these trees. See where the grass is roughed up? Right about here."

She put down the lamp and stuck her rusty spade into the damp earth. A hazy, cool chill in the air made their jackets feel damp as they began to dig into the small mound of earth. It wasn't long before Margie struck something solid with her shovel and after another load of dirt she found a piece of burlap, the kind that gave the impression of many years of use.

"Um, Dots...I think I found him."

The stench of death hit them with full force and both gagged as they stepped back from the grave. Gathering themselves at a safe distance, their stomachs recovered and they moved back to the task of verifying the corpse.

Each shovel full of dirt exposed more of the bundle and Dotsie suddenly moved back from the pile and dropped her tool. Her hands moved up to her face and she began to sob quietly, her body shaking lightly with each heavy breath.

"Are you alright Dots?" her best friend asked as she moved to comfort the sobs.

There was no answer, only more soft crying and Margie put her hand on Dotsie's shoulder to give consolation. The young girl's grief gradually subsided and Margie looked her best friend in her eyes.

"I didn't think this would bother me." Dotsie whispered.

"He was going to kill Jonah and me...I swear it. I had to do it. I had to do it."

"What do you mean...you had to do it? You did it? Not Jonah?"

The incredulous look on Margie's face made Dotsie tear up again.

"Jonah didn't kill him... I did. He was going to kill Jonah and I had my dad's pistol. I had to do it."

The incredulous expression turned to one of compassion. They embraced again and then took up the task of a messy, obvious reburial. Averting their eyes, they made a mental note of the exact location where Hunter Carlyle lay.

The women moved quietly back along the way they came, the light extinguished to avoid detection after their task. The moon was thin, but walking along the tree line gave them a small amount of guidance and before they knew it, they were back in Dotsie's yard.

"Dots, how is anyone going to find that body?"

"It's easy. We can put together a little note, sloppily written, and then drop it tomorrow night in Sheriff Johnson's mailbox. No one will be the wiser and he will be given the directions to the body. We just can't get caught with the note. You can drop it."

"Me? I'm going to drop it? Why ME?"

"If I get caught dropping it, they will tie me to Jonah. They won't tie you to him. Besides, you won't get caught...I will be just out of sight to help you. I can be your lookout."

The next day came and went and both women were standing on a side street near the middle of the small town, acting as nonchalant as possible. They appeared to just be two girls out for a casual stroll on a calm, midsummer evening. Dotsie slowly moved across the quiet street and suddenly lagged slightly behind her friend.

Margie moved quietly with quickness in her step and took the small envelope from the side pocket of her sweater. In one swift motion, she opened the metal swing door to the mailbox quickly and slid the note in. A quick look to the left and right followed and seeing no one near, she closed the door quietly and kept moving up the street. She crossed over to the other side and continued moving along with her friend by her side. No one was the wiser.

"Nice work, girl. You could be one of those spies in those drug store books!"

Dotsie gave her friend a gentle, victorious smile.

"Yeah, right. A spy. Gee whiz Dots, I think I peed myself back there!"

Both girls chuckled and locked arms as only young girls do, both feeling high from the success of their adventure.

Chapter Fifteen

Helen Anderson always arrived before her boss because she believed it was the proper thing to do. Responsible punctuality was becoming a lost art in these times. Dedication was important when you worked for the highest lawman in the land, or at least in their little town.

She stopped by the small mailbox out front of the station and grabbed three pieces of mail which she set on the same corner of Sheriff Johnson's desk every morning. Carefully unfolding the local news of the day, she noted that another family in town was about to lose their farm to foreclosure. Her boss had made a visit with a warning a couple of days before. Banks could be cruel, cold, and totally heartless. They used law enforcement as their messenger. It seemed to Helen to be a cowardice move.

Tom Johnson arrived promptly at eight o'clock to begin another dreadful day of issuing bank warnings and occasionally escorting families off their property. He saw his mail waiting for him and, as he was about to grab the small pile and search the contents, he heard the front bell on the door jingle as someone entered their lobby.

"Albert Crenshaw, what can I do for you?"

"Good morning, Mrs. Anderson. Is the new sheriff in?"

The elderly professional tilted her head toward the office on her left and smiled at her visitor, a kid that she liked for as long as she could remember.

"Sheriff Johnson is in there. You can go right in."

The young man paused for a moment and then turned back to the lady behind the desk.

"Has he figured out who killed all those people the other night? Somebody said it was faulty wiring, but I think I saw the escaped kid wandering around. I'm betting he set the building on fire."

The old lady's expression turned from a smile to one of horror.

"You saw the kid? The one Hunter was chasing? When? Where? You had better tell the sheriff right away!"

Albert nodded and, with a sense of mission, suddenly left the room and entered the sheriff's office.

"What can I do for you, young man?"

This was the first time that Sheriff Johnson entertained a visitor in his office and he felt a small air of importance. He gestured to his visitor to take a seat and he sat down behind his oak desk.

"Sheriff, there is something you should know about. That fire at the town hall the other night was not an accident. I saw the transient kid around the building and I'm positive that he started the fire. I'm sure that he's killed Hunter Carlyle too. The kid is still around and I think we are all in danger. I think he's crazy...a lunatic."

A half hour of questions and answers flew between them and the sheriff knew what he had to do. After cordially dismissing his guest, he began to organize a posse to make a run out to the farm and old barn on the edge of town. If the guest of honor was still present he would be apprehended and tried for his crimes.

Albert Crenshaw walked out to the main lobby and out of the front door. Then Johnson remembered his initial task and returned his attention to his mail.

A small, white envelope... doesn't look like a bill or summons. Wonder what this is?

****

A group of eight remaining elders gathered together with their weapons from home and followed Sheriff Johnson out to the old farm. The house that once stood proudly on the acreage was now nothing but a rocky foundation. The moon lit their way from the dilapidated structure to the door of the barn.

Moving with caution, they entered and searched the premises with no luck. It was apparent that someone had been there recently but no one remained.

Kerosine lanterns gave off an eerie, flickering glow as the men continued to search the premises with no success. The group fanned out in widening circles and began combing the property for clues. Sheriff Johnson directed the group as best as he could while reviewing the contents of the letter in his mind.

The letter said the kid is buried out here somewhere along the tree line, near the brook south of the old barn. Look for a shallow grave. Maybe this is a hoax.

The determined silence was broken by someone near the edge of the woods fifty yards away. Johnson hurried over to the man, careful not to trip in the darkened night.

"Uh, Sheriff? You might want to take a look at this."

The man held his lantern close to the ground and Johnson recognized the discovery immediately. The sudden stench and degradation made him take a quick step backwards. They stood over Hunter Carlyle's grave.

Chapter Sixteen

"I must go to the funeral, if I don't show up people will suspect us. Everything needs to look normal."

"You don't think that Albert has betrayed you, do you? That they will apprehend you when you show up?"

Dotsie turned away for a moment as she contemplated her role in the situation.

"No, Albert would not implicate me...he likes me. Maybe likes me too much. He's not going to turn me over to the law and he doesn't know that I shot Hunter. He won't turn on me, instead he's turned on you and wants to be a hero. You need to worry, not me."

The funeral for Hunter Carlyle was scheduled for early in the evening as the days were much too hot to have an indoor event such as this. Dotsie showed up with her best friend, Margie, and felt sick to her stomach the minute she stepped into the old, stuffy building.

The entryway held an elevated table with a guestbook, and she signed it slowly with a trembling hand. Beyond two open heavy oak doors was the parlor itself and she caught a glimpse of the coffin at the front of the parlor. A quiet entrance gave way to quiet sobbing and whispers as she moved off to the side of the room. There was no way she could bear to look at the closed coffin. Decomposition ruled out a final look at the body for those present and she was slightly relieved to not have to see Hunter's face.

A few classmates wandered over and quiet sympathies were exchanged, but no one really knew how to act in a situation such as this. It was one thing for old people to die and there had been plenty of funerals after the town hall fire, but this was different. The dead person was young, a classmate, one of them.

Then she saw him, standing alone along the wall on the other side of the parlor. His gaze, fixed toward her, lingered way too long. He was staring, almost stalking her. Before she could react he was within ten feet of her, approaching with confidence, but in a weird way.

"Hi Albert."

"Such a shame, isn't it? Hunter gone at the hands of that killer. He was one of us and the stranger took him away."

An uncomfortable silence lingered after his last words and he shook his head back and forth in condemnation of the act.

"You wouldn't happen to know where the killer is, would you Dotsie?"

The words were both quiet and threatening and Dotsie looked around the room with hopes that no one overheard the question.

"Come on, Albert. I know as much as you do. I couldn't begin to have any idea where Jonah disappeared to. One minute he was in the barn, the next he was gone."

She feared that her response wasn't convincing enough and shrugged while looking away.

"You mean to tell me that you have not seen Jonah since we met in the barn the night of the fire?"

The imposing stare from the inquisitioner was powerful and Dotsie wished she was anywhere else.

"Albert, I know as much as you do. First my dad and grandpa, and now this. I don't know how much more I can take."

Dotsie turned to the door, grabbed Margie by the elbow, and made a quick exit with tears in her eyes. To Albert it appeared genuine, but Dotsie was silently impressed with her acting and thought that an Academy Award would befit her.

"What was that all about?"

Dotsie turned to her friend as they walked down the main street of town and gave a small smile.

"Just surviving. Keeping Albert at bay."

Margie stopped and turned to face her friend.

"You know he's on to you, right? He suspects that you and Jonah are still a couple and he is jealous as hell. You have to watch out for him."

"Have you told him anything about us?"

The smile was gone from her face, replaced with accusation.

"No, Dots. I would never do that. But he knows something is up. You have been avoiding the group and he suspects it's because of Jonah. He's watching you. Be careful."

Dotsie didn't need the strict warning but appreciated the genuine care her friend was showing. She knew Albert well enough to never trust him and now a hatred was brewing inside of her. She had welcomed him into their friendship circle and now he was betraying her. It just proved to her that one good deed could be costly when it comes to building friendships.

****

The best friends quietly entered the house and both plopped down on Margie's large feather bed. With a shared giggle, the words began to flow.

"Does he love you?"

"Margie, how should I know? It's not like we talk about that kind of stuff."

The curious friend pried further.

"Come on, Dots. Do you love him?"

This question brought a blush to Dotsie's face. Her eyes connected with her best friend's and she giggled lightly with a sense of nervousness.

"Dotsie, if you can't tell me who can you tell...I'm your best friend!"

A soft smile appeared on the teen's face as she nodded slowly.

"I think I love him. He is so handsome! I get nervous around him but when we begin to talk everything is so comfortable, so exciting yet wonderful. I can't quite describe it, it's so natural. It's like we are meant to be."

Margie sat up straight and looked her friend in the eyes. Slightly jealous, she was however very happy for her best friend.

"You are in love, girl...plain and simple. Have you told him you love him?"

A shyness emanated with Dotsie's reply.

"Tell Jonah I love him? I can't do that...it will scare him away. He hasn't told me and he should tell me first, don't you think?"

"I don't think there are any hard and fast rules on who is supposed to tell who when it comes to romance. If he loves you he will tell you when the time is right. Right?"

Both girls sat in silence for a moment pondering the new situation.

"Do you think he will tell me?"

Margie laughed with a broad smile.

"Oh, he will tell you alright. What will you say when it happens?"

"I don't know. I have had boys ask me out but none have ever said they were in love with me. I sure hope that I don't go and do something foolish... you know, like start crying or something."

"Well, I'm not an expert in this field. I have yet to find someone that I really love, but I know this. When the time is right, you will be radiant and will say the right thing. I just know it."

The girls spent another hour together talking about everything imaginable and then said goodbye with a long, heartfelt hug.

Chapter Seventeen

"Jonah, I'm going into town for more groceries. Is there anything you want?"

The request woke him suddenly and he was not eager to rise from the comfort of the bed. The sun was up but Jonah could not get a feel for what time of day it was. His response was sleepy and curt.

"Nothing. I'm too tired to think."

Dotsie laughed at the bottom of the stairs.

"How about a six pack of beer?"

This made Jonah laugh.

"Sure."

"Yeah, you bet...hotshot! Keep dreaming!"

They both laughed at her comment and Dotsie walked quickly out the front door and down the porch steps with her purse in hand.

It seemed like a minute had passed but in reality, it was more like a half hour when the front door suddenly opened and a soft, female voice called out.

"Anyone here?"

Jonah's mind snapped to attention and after a second call out from below he recognized the voice as Margie's.

"Up here." He replied as he sat up and pulled on a shirt and pants.

"Hey, are you just waking up?"

Her smile caught his attention right away and he returned a sleepy grin.

"You know you don't have to get dressed on account of me. I won't mind."

The sexiness of her voice and the flirtatious offer was shocking, but also a pleasant surprise and his posture became more confident.

"What would your friend say if she heard you say that?" he countered with a flair of humor and challenge.

"Dotsie's not here. It's just you and me."

An alarm went off deep in his mind that told him to get out of the situation as fast as possible, but he chose to ignore it for the moment.

Margie looked much too good to resist. Her summer dress gave away her womanly features and Jonah found himself tempted and temporarily speechless.

She moved to the bed and sat down next to him. He moved slightly to give her a comfortable place to sit. She smiled and touched his arm softly. Her touch felt heavenly.

"What Dotsie doesn't know won't hurt her, will it? Can you keep a secret?"

Jonah gulped slightly and nodded, not knowing what to do next.

"I think you are very good looking, and I have noticed you looking at me. I think we could have some fun, know what I mean?"

Margie then moved close and her face was inches away from his. He could smell her delicate perfume and could feel her warm breath on his face. She put both arms around his neck and waited for him to make the next move. A passionate kiss was expected.

"Um, Margie...we can't do this. It just isn't right."

Jonah stammered with embarrassment, feeling less of a man by not taking her right there.

"It's not that I don't want you, believe me you are so beautiful, so...you know. It's just that I can't hurt her. Truth be told, I love Dotsie. I have never loved anyone like the way I love her."

Margie pulled her arms from around his neck and slowly slid away from him. Their eyes met and her smile was genuine.

"I'm sorry I did this, Jonah. I hope you will forgive me. I guess I just got caught up in the moment. I'm sorry. I'm happy for you and Dotsie."

Her voice was soft but panicked and held a flavor of embarrassment that was both sad and cute.

"You won't tell Dotsie about this, will you?"

Jonah reached out and touched her arm in a friendly gesture.

"Don't worry about this, Margie. I won't ever say anything...this will be our secret. You know, I'm actually very flattered."

Margie made her way down the stairs and out the door and Jonah let out a loud gasp as he fell back onto the bed with both hands behind his head.

Damn, what a crazy way to start the day! Holy cow!

****

"Well, how did it go?"

Margie shut the door to her room and bounced onto her bed with a smile. The young women found themselves right back where they were the day before and Dotsie's curiosity was killing her.

"He loves you alright, no doubt about it!"

"No, you're kidding me...this isn't funny!"

"Dots, I'm serious! I put on my best charm, over did the sexuality, totally put the moves on him. I sat on the bed with him and even moved in for a romantic kiss and he didn't do anything. He actually moved away a little as I held on around his neck. Then he said it...he said it all. He LOVES you, Dots!"

Dotsie looked at her friend and had a mixture of emotions. Did anything happen between her and Jonah? Was she seriously trying to steal him away?

"Margie, you weren't trying to steal him away from me were you?"

The question popped out of her mouth suddenly and the minute she said it she wished she could take it back. A look of alarm, and then pain, took hold of Margie's face. Her head slowly moved back and forth, indicating the negative, and her gaze dropped to the bed.

"Dotsie, I'm your best friend. Trust me, I would never do that to you. I love you too. We both agreed to test this out. We agreed to put Jonah to the test, and he passed. He loves you...he said he's never loved anyone the way he loves you."

The silence was deafening and a tear ran down Margie's face.

"I'm so sorry, Margie. I'm sorry I asked that...that I thought that. I never should have said or believed that you would betray me. Margie, you are my best friend...you will always be my best friend. Please forgive me."

Her friend looked up and wiped away the tear.

"Do you really think Jonah would ever leave you for me? Are you crazy? You're so beautiful. If he had leaned to kiss me, I would have backed away and left. Dots, you must know that, you must believe me. I will never hurt you."

Both girls leaned into each other with a long hug and a few shared tears. They both knew at that moment that they would always be best friends. Then Dotsie backed away with a sudden smile toward her friend.

"Oh my god, Margie, what should I do? He loves me!"

Chapter Eighteen

Dotsie made the trek east of town to her place and noticed that the house was completely dark as she entered.

"Good, he's being careful."

After shutting the front door tightly and locking the deadbolt, she walked to the edge of the stairs.

"Jonah? Are you here?"

Her whisper made him smile as he moved from her room to the top of the stairs.

"I'm right up here, Dots. Is everything all right?"

"Yes, but let's get upstairs quickly. I think Albert is watching the house...looking for you. Stay away from the windows and stay quiet. He can hear you if he's standing in the back yard."

What little moonlight that existed cast an eerie glow upon the old farmhouse and sent shivers through the young sheriff. He had worked late at night before, but this felt different. The darkness enveloped him to the core and aside from the quiet chirping of cicadas along the road, there was a silence that hinted of danger.

Johnson patiently scanned the front of the dwelling from across a dirt road, partially hidden in a ditch. The heat from earlier in the day hung in the air and he could smell and taste dust from the surface in front of him.

Hardly a light on. Does the girl even live here anymore? It's so quiet. She left the funeral with her friend the other day...maybe they didn't come back here.

With a slow, deliberate pace the sheriff moved around the house to the back lot by the barn and looked up to find a single light on the second floor along with a quick shadow moving along the partially open curtain. He wasn't sure, but he thought that the image was a little too large to be a woman.

Johnson waited for a while longer, standing in the shadow of the barn so as not be detected. Then he moved back to the front of the house and approached the threshold with care.

The knock at the front door startled both Dotsie and Jonah and he reached for the lamp to turn it off. Their eyes met in a moment of fear and then the girl put her index finger to her lips.

"Hide. Don't make a sound. It's probably Albert."

Her voice a whisper, she pointed toward her closet. Jonah felt his stomach stir with anxiety, a feeling of dread creeping over him. He slid into the small space and closed the door carefully.

Dotsie cautiously descended the staircase to the entryway, trying to see who was standing on the stoop. The figure was too large to be Albert and so she straightened up a bit and took a deep breath to bring her racing heart back to normal. Flipping on the front porch light, she looked through the curtained window and saw a large figure. She recognized Sheriff Johnson.

Opening the door with as much poise as she could muster, Dotsie put on a smile that would charm the coldest of individuals. She didn't need to win over the sheriff because he returned her smile while admiring her soft beauty. A tense situation dissipated with a very warm greeting.

"Good evening, I'm Sheriff Johnson...the new guy in town."

"Yes, I recognize you. You have your work quite cut out for you, huh?"

They shared a gentle chuckle and then he continued with warm purpose.

"Mind if I come in and ask you a few questions?"

Dotsie stepped back, slightly shaken with his demand, and then quickly composed herself. The sheriff took quiet notice of her actions.

"No, I don't mind at all. Please come in."

The officer moved through the doorway with his hat in his hand and carefully closed the door behind him.

"What can I do for you?" the young woman stammered slightly as she now moved with a soft clumsiness.

"How foolish of me...please take a seat. Can I get you anything to drink? Water?"

Her hands shook slightly and so she clasped them together in front of her. This also caught the attention of the lawman.

Hmm. Looks like she might be hiding something...or someone.

"No thank you, nothing for me."

He paused for a moment to let the importance of his presence sink in and then he cut to the chase.

"You're Dorothy Gravelle, right?"

"My friends call me Dotsie."

"Dotsie...that's a pretty name. We have a bit of a problem here. You see I know that you are hiding a young man here in your house and he could possibly be the killer of the young man whose funeral took place yesterday. I need to talk to him...please bring him to me."

The direct approach sent the young woman's mind reeling and she didn't know how to respond. The look of alarm and confusion captured her expression.

"Look, I need to talk with him and I know he's upstairs. You can bring him down to me or I will have to go up and get him. It's your choice. I only want to talk to him."

Dotsie's shoulders dropped in defeat as she knew they had been found out. She couldn't process how or why quite yet but she sensed a dangerous urgency if she did not comply with the sheriff.

"I will go get him. His name is Jonah and he has done nothing wrong. He's being framed. He has done absolutely nothing wrong, understand?"

"I'm not accusing him of anything. I just want to talk to him."

A moment later Jonah appeared in the front room, visibly scared. His eyes never moved from the lawman and he fought the temptation to bolt from the house into the darkness to disappear forever. Common sense and his love for Dotsie took hold of his senses, and he sat down slowly across from the sheriff.

"I have reason to believe that you were involved in the disappearance and murder of Hunter Carlyle. Can you tell me anything that would dispel this notion?"

"Sir, I had nothing to do with Hunter Carlyle. He was hunting me...trying to kill me. This weird, crazy thing you guys have going on here where you execute people over in the park is the reason that I was running from him. He was going to kill me! You know that, I'm sure."

The sheriff gazed from Jonah to Dotsie and then back as he answered as tactfully as he could.

"I just found out about this ritual, this thing at the park. I'm new here. I swear that I didn't know about this until after the fire at the old town hall. My assistant told me about it. I will certainly be putting a stop to this thing. But tell me...did you have something to do with Hunter's demise?"

"No sir, I didn't kill Hunter."

Johnson studied his expression for a long moment and detected a degree of truth, but he still had an inclination that the young man knew more than he was letting on.

"I have it on good knowledge that you were hiding out in the old barn on County Road 3. There are people that can place you there around the approximate time of Hunter's disappearance. We were given additional knowledge that led us to the barn and we recovered Hunter's body out there in a shallow grave. It seems to me that you are a logical suspect in this whole thing. Can you change my mind?"

Dotsie suddenly spoke up, changing the interrogation's tone to one that matched her alarm and temper.

"Did Albert Crenshaw put you up to this? Was he telling you garbage about Jonah? He hates Jonah, you know. He is jealous of Jonah because Jonah and I are in love. Albert has a thing for me, always has, and I don't like him. Now Albert is trying to destroy Jonah and me. Albert Crenshaw can't be trusted...Albert Crenshaw is a liar!"

The room instantly fell silent, the echo of the young woman's plea the only thing echoing in their ears. The sheriff looked at the couple and felt that they were being truthful. He knew he didn't have enough evidence to arrest the young man, but that reality could change quickly enough.

"Oh, one last thing. Where were you the day that Hunter was killed?"

Chapter Nineteen

"You told the sheriff that we were in love. Did you mean it?"

The question hung in the air. A soft smile crossed Dotsie's face and Jonah didn't need an answer, her expression said it all.

"Yes. I meant it. I love you. Do you love me?"

Her question was barely out of her mouth before Jonah answered.

"I have never loved anybody until you. Yes, I love you."

The young couple moved to each other in a passionate embrace. Suddenly everything was right in the world.

****

Tom Johnson tried his best to get the young man to crumble with his last question but now he felt that he had been outsmarted. He had tried to set Jonah up in hopes that he would trip over his answer and give information away.

I don't think the kid did it, but who else would? He should have bitten at the reference of where he was on the day of, but he didn't budge. He didn't indicate that he knew the day that Hunter died. He could very well have been at the young woman's home the whole time. I don't have any way to pin the kid down.

The short walk back to the downtown area and his station gave him time to work through his thought process concerning what he had heard. The rookie sheriff became frustrated at the fact that he couldn't get more out of the young couple. They seemed genuine and now he had little information or clues to proceed with as he continued to investigate the murder of Hunter Carlyle.

The townspeople are going to hang my ass if I don't get something going quickly.

His eyes suddenly caught the movement of a figure moving toward him on the opposite side of the road. He moved to the cover of trees and watched as the figure approached with a deliberate stride. As the distance closed between them, the pale moonlight illuminated the person.

"Albert Crenshaw." He quietly murmured to himself.

The figure passed and he moved slowly along the tree line to follow the young man without being detected. The pair moved all the way back to Dotsie's house and Albert had no idea he was being trailed. As they came upon the farm the sheriff made his move.

"Good evening, Albert. How are you? What brings you out here tonight?"

Crenshaw stepped back, obviously startled, and panic crossed his face.

"Um, hey Sheriff. I'm just out for a walk and I was going to stop in to see Dotsie...to see if she is all right. She's a friend of mine and times have been tough for her lately with her dad, grandpa, and Hunter...you know?"

The young man was spilling information in a defensive state, not a good sign for a person out for a casual walk.

"You are friends with Dotsie, huh?"

"Yes sir. Real close."

"How close, Albert?"

Crenshaw swayed from one side to the other slightly, his nerves betraying him.

"Real close. We have known each other for a long time. You could say she is my girlfriend."

The sense of bravado took over and Albert was now trying his best to show off for the older man.

Real close? The girl just said how she was in love with this Jonah kid and now she suddenly has a boyfriend right here? She said he was jealous of her and Jonah...hmmm.

"Albert, I have an idea. Dotsie probably doesn't want to be disturbed tonight, with her situation at home and the funeral and all. I just stopped over to her house and checked on her myself and she's going to be fine. What do you say we walk back into town together? It would be nice to have some company."

"Sir, I should really check on her. She is expecting me. It's pretty important."

"No Albert, let's go back to town. She is fine, you can check on her tomorrow."

The look that Johnson shot at Albert gave an intense impression that he would not take no for an answer, that he meant business.

"Let's go."

Albert dutifully turned around and moved next to the lawman on his way down the dirt road.

"You know what I think, Sheriff? I think that this new kid in town, Jonah something or other, killed Hunter. I think he burned the town hall and I think he will kill again. Do you know where he is?"

The sheriff turned his eyes from the dirt road in the distance to look Crenshaw over. He slowed his pace a bit and then smiled at the young man.

"You know, Albert, I have no idea where this Jonah kid could be. He could be anywhere. What makes you think that he killed Hunter?"

Albert realized that he suddenly had the lawman's ear and he perked up with excitement and conviction.

"The way I see it this is simple. The kid comes into town and nobody knows him. He could be killing people all over the place, from one town to the next. He's on the run from the police."

Johnson stopped and turned about face to study Albert more as the young man's theory flowed out with intensity. He had heard a version of this from the young man before. The question was whether Albert could keep his story up.

"Go on."

"Well the way I see it is Jonah was jealous of Hunter, he probably thought that Hunter was Dotsie's boyfriend. He sees Dotsie and falls in love with her. Then he decides to stick around and he kills his rival, who is Hunter, with the hope of winning her over.

It's pretty simple. He then creates a bigger stir by burning up the town hall and killing more people. He's a vial, cold blooded killer, plain and simple."

Albert looked the sheriff in the eyes and nodded his head for added effect.

"Well, you might be on to something here. It would certainly explain some of what has gone on here over the last week or more. Now I have something to think about. Thank you, Albert."

With that last statement the two began to walk again and were standing on Main Street five minutes later.

One thing is for sure. This kid is involved in this somehow. Maybe the girl is right...he might be chasing her and clearing the way by killing his rivals. This kid is nuttier than a Christmas fruitcake.

Chapter Twenty

"Hey Albert, what are you up to?"

Margie put on a sultry show and Albert did a double take when he locked eyes with her. Her voice was soft and her look was alluring. Albert wasn't used to experiencing a young woman's attention in this manner.

"I'm just finishing up trimming my mom's hedges, hard work on a hot day."

He smiled with as much charm as he could muster as he swaggered closer to the young woman standing in the shade of the oak tree close by.

"I find that a man who does outdoor work is impressive...sexy in a certain way."

The young man almost dropped his hedge sheers as he couldn't believe what Margie was saying.

"I work outside a lot." he responded while sticking out his chest in a manly act.

Margie had everything she could do to not laugh out loud at this silly act, but she didn't want to offend Albert. It was obvious that he had never been propositioned by anyone before.

"I don't suppose you would want to take an evening stroll around town with me sometime, huh? After all, I would guess you would rather hang out with Dotsie, right? It is a shame, I think we could have a good time, what with summer coming to an end and all."

Margie stared him down and gently flipped her long brown curls over her shoulder with her hand. The young coquette knew exactly what she was doing.

Albert stepped forward a stride and stopped to judge whether she was serious or playing a joke on him. Margie had never shown a real interest in him before and now he wondered what had changed.

"Are you serious Margie, or are you putting me on?"

The young woman's sultry smile turned to a pained frown and he knew he had crossed a line with his statement. She now looked hurt.

"Of course I am serious. Do you think I would intentionally hurt anyone? Do you think I would hurt you? I just thought we could spend some time together and maybe get to know each other a little more."

Albert cocked his head to the side and smiled with newfound confidence.

"I'm sorry if I offended you, I didn't mean to. Honestly. I would like to hang out with you...to go for a walk with you sometime and maybe even a show. Will you forgive me?"

Margie moved forward with a cautious grace, put her right hand on his bicep, and gave him a gentle kiss on the cheek. Albert could feel himself blush as she slowly pulled away with a smile.

"Take me for a walk tonight? Say seven o'clock? Pick me up at my house...don't be late.

Albert watched her saunter away and he couldn't help but beam with pride. Margie had matured from a girl to a woman over the summer and he took a moment to check her out as she swayed down the boulevard.

Margie has certainly grown up. Damn.

****

Seven o'clock could not come quick enough for Albert Crenshaw and he found himself jogging the three blocks to Margie's house. He slowed to a normal pace when her home came into sight and he was surprised to see her sitting on the front stoop.

Albert was wearing his Sunday best and had even combed his hair with pomade to make it shine and look regal. He did a double take when he saw Margie. She was absolutely stunning. Her white dress with blue polka-dots reached over her knees and projected her sensuality. Her hair was radiant and he could barely get words out of his mouth.

"Hi Margie, nice night for a walk, huh?"

The young woman giggled lightly at the comment that gave away his nerves.

"Yes, Albert. A nice night for a walk."

She stood up and he took in all her beauty as she spun toward the screen door and called out to her father.

"Daddy, I'm going downtown for a walk with Albert, alright?"

A deep voice emanated from somewhere inside the dwelling and it scared Albert.

"Don't be gone long, young lady. Be home before it gets dark!"

A burly man appeared in the doorway, and he did not look pleased at the fact that his young girl was in the presence of a young man.

"Don't be silly, Daddy. Of course I will be home before dark."

The father took another moment to stare down Albert. The fright on the suitor's face was evident as the couple turned and made their way down to the boulevard.

A quarter of a block later Albert could finally speak up.

"Your dad is scary."

"Don't be silly, Albert. He's just trying to scare you so that you don't take advantage of me. You wouldn't take advantage of me, would you?"

The way she asked the question excited him; it was as if she were asking him to make a move on her.

"Not unless you want me too." he replied with a playful, hopeful smile.

Margie giggled and reached out to take his hand in hers as they slowly walked around the corner to Main Street. Approaching them on the sidewalk was Dotsie with a bag of grocery items. She almost dropped the bag when they came into view.

"Hi Dots, shopping huh?" Margie greeted with a smile.

Albert stood back from the two, obviously uncomfortable with what was taking place. He wanted Dotsie but suddenly was fixated on her best friend Margie. In his mind, this could not turn out well.

"Hey Margie. Yes, I suddenly needed to make a grocery trip… my cupboards are bare."

The girls chuckled in a friendly manner, but Dotsie kept looking at Albert and he couldn't move his gaze from her.

"Al and I are just out for a walk. I'd ask you to join us but you look like you have your hands full."

"You are right about that. Have fun you two."

Dotsie hurried away, looking back once or twice. Margie turned to Albert, took his hand again, and continued down the sidewalk that fronted small local shops. Occasional waves and greetings were exchanged with friends and acquaintances and Albert felt himself becoming more comfortable with each step.

With a pride-filled expression, he greeted and waved at almost everybody he could in an effort to be noticed. A pretty girl on one's arm could turn an average person into someone special and Albert noticed all the males checking his out his girl. He decided to take a chance.

"You know you're beautiful right? Look at everyone staring at you...they are all taken by your beauty."

The comment took Margie by surprise and she stopped to look him in the eyes. She was suddenly caught up in his comment and presence.

"You are being silly. They are looking at both of us."

"I think you are wrong, Margie, in fact I know you are wrong. You are absolutely beautiful."

The young woman openly blushed and pushed her hair back across her shoulder. She studied Albert intently and realized that he was serious.

"Thank you, Al. I don't know what to say."

"Don't say anything, Margie. Just stay with me."

Margie changed the subject to small talk as they moved among the storefronts, checking out the merchandise windows and commenting on their value. Time flew by and before they knew it dusk was falling.

"We had better get back to my house...it is getting dark and my dad will kill both of us if we don't get there quickly."

"You don't have to tell me twice. Your dad WILL kill me!"

As they reached the front steps of Margie's house Albert leaned in for a kiss. Margie moved her head to the side and kissed him on the cheek in an effort to be a proper lady and not move too quickly. Soft words were exchanged and Albert made his way back home, as high as a kite.

Margie's eyes followed him down the street as she watched from the large front room window. When he finally disappeared around the corner, she ran to her dad.

"Daddy, I'm going to run out to Dotsie's house really quick. I promise I will be back soon."

"Be careful out there. Don't go to visit that boy, understand?"

"No sir. Just going to Dotsie's."

She bolted out the back door, across the yard to the alley, and then out the side street toward the Gravelle place and her best friend. Removing her fancy shoes, she ran as fast as she could and surprised herself with how fast she moved.

Margie slowed when she got to the front door and put her fancy shoes back on. It didn't seem proper in her mind to carry them, they were made to impress by being worn. She knocked three times on the weathered, wooden front door and after a moment Dotsie answered.

"Nice work, Margie. I was impressed...you are quite the lady. I barely recognized you with the makeup!"

Margie entered the dated living room and plopped down on a sofa that had seen much better days. It creaked loudly when she settled into it. Dotsie's curiosity was killing her.

"So tell me girl, how did it go?"

"Where's Jonah?"

"He's upstairs sleeping like a baby. He won't bother us. Tell me Margie...how did it go with Al?"

Margie rolled her eyes and let out a loud laugh.

"He's such a clumsy putz. He's so awkward around me...he doesn't even know how to talk!"

"What did he tell you about me?"

"About you? He was on a date with me and I do believe he was smitten. You're not going to believe this. He actually told me I was beautiful!"

Margie turned her eyes away for a moment and Dotsie started to laugh.

"What's so funny? You don't think I'm beautiful?"

"Don't you see it? He's falling for you! Albert Crenshaw is falling in love with you!"

"He doesn't like me...you're crazy! You think this is funny, don't you?"

"Albert Crenshaw is in love with you or at least smitten on you. You are capturing his heart. I can't blame him, Margie, you are beautiful."

"You really think so, Dots?"

"You're beautiful, Margie, and you are a beautiful friend."

Dotsie paused a moment to let the statement sink in and then she continued with excitement.

"So tell me...what did he say?"

"I don't know. He didn't say much. He just kept looking at me and smiling. It was kind of creepy."

Dotsie laughed out loud again at her friend.

"Is this the first time any boy has given you any attention?"

Margie fell silent and looked down at her lap.

"Yes. The boys don't look at me like they look at you."

Her friend rolled her eyes and smiled.

"Get used to it, Margie...you are the next big thing. All the boys will be checking you out...mark my words...they will all be chasing you. You had better get used to it."

This statement brought a wide smile from the newest pretty girl in town.

Chapter Twenty One

The knock came very early on a Saturday morning and the sharpness of it brought both people out of a deep sleep. Jonah looked across the pillow at Dotsie and nodded as she got out of bed and headed toward the door.

Moving slowly down the stairs, she noticed the large figure on the other side of the curtains and realized that the police were back. Checking the front of her nightgown for modesty, she paused a moment and then opened the door to greet the sheriff.

"Good morning, Dotsie, can I come in?"

"Um, sure I guess."

"Is Jonah here? I need to talk to him."

"What do you need to talk to him about?"

"I'd rather talk to him directly...can you get him for me?"

Panic overcame her mind and she felt the impulse to lie and save her lover.

"He's not here right now. He went out."

Her eyes shifted downward and the officer knew she wasn't truthful.

"Come on, Dotsie. I know he's here. I just need to talk to him."

His look conveyed a seriousness that the girl could not avoid. She turned her gaze to the top of the stairs and with reluctant surrender, she called out to Jonah.

He appeared at the top of the stairs and, noticing the lawman, he was resigned to the fact that he was probably going into town.

"Hi Jonah. I need to talk to you; this is very important."

"Go ahead. Say what you have to say."

"I'm going to have to take you into custody...it's for your own good, believe me. I know you didn't kill the kid, or at least I am pretty sure you didn't. The elders that remain in town have figured out that you are here and if they get a hold of you it will not be good. They have already convicted you in their minds and they will be stringing up a rope for you. If I take you into custody they cannot harm you. You will be under my protection and eventually the charges against you will run out of time. At that point I can release you and I will take you out of the county. You will be able to get away."

Jonah turned his attention to his lover. He could see that she was distraught and on the verge of crying. He turned back to the sheriff.

"What if I told you that I didn't want to leave, to get away? What if I told you that I wanted to stay here with Dotsie? Can I really trust you when everyone in town wants you to capture me? How do I know you're not going to take me in and be the hero?"

Tom Johnson turned to Dotsie and realized that she was nodding in agreement with her man. He focused back on Jonah.

"I don't know what to tell you that will make you believe me. All I can say is that they are coming for you and if they find you, they will finish you. It could be the rope, it could be the gun, but I won't be able to stop them if they get you first. You have to believe me; your best chance is to come with me."

Jonah moved to Dotsie and hugged her like he had never hugged anyone before. The tears flowed as she sobbed uncontrollably and he tried to comfort her.

"It's going to be alright, Dots. I believe in Sheriff Johnson. I will be safe and this will all be over soon."

He turned to the sheriff as he held his girlfriend.

"One thing you need to know. I am not going to leave this town without Dotsie. I will NEVER leave her here alone...NEVER."

The sheriff nodded in understanding.

"Fair enough, you don't have to leave but you need to come with me to be safe. Dotsie can visit you whenever you want and this won't take long, but I need you to believe me and come into custody. I will keep you safe, even if I need to sleep in the jail with a shotgun on my lap."

Jonah turned to Dotsie, gave her a hug and a long, passionate kiss, and then followed the lawman out the door. They walked into town, looking left, right, forward, and behind for any threats that might show up. The town was still fast asleep as they made their way into the sheriff's office and into the jail. Jonah was in custody, being held for questioning and, as far as Sheriff Johnson was concerned, the less that the townspeople knew the better. Word spread through the town and by noon a crowd was already starting to gather.

"C'mon, Sheriff...let him out so that we can handle this the right way! He's a killer! Hunter's family needs to get their dues! Let him out!"

The sheriff shook his head left and right and with a sly grin on his face he answered the crowd.

"NOBODY IS LEAVING ANY JAIL CELLS AND YOU ARE NOT GETTING IN. I WILL ARREST EVERY LAST ONE OF YOU WHO TRIES TO DEFY THE LEGAL SYSTEM!"

The crowd tried to no avail as it became obvious that the sheriff was turning no one over to the public any time soon.

When the crowd finally dispersed, Tom Johnson went back to the jail area and sat down in front of Jonah's cell.

"Tell me Jonah, why in the world did you come into this place and why in the hell do you want to stay?"

It didn't take Jonah long to construct an answer because he decided to be truthful with the sheriff.

"I jumped a train back in Indiana to head west. I damn nears got killed by an old drunk and three other thieves and then I ended up jumping off the train here. Next thing I knew some kid wanted to kill me and so I made a run for it. I met Dotsie and she took me to a barn outside of town and you know the rest. Here I am."

The sheriff paused a moment and studied his prisoner, realizing that the story was probably true.

"Did you kill the kid? Hunter Carlyle?"

Jonah looked at Johnson and shook his head.

"No way, sir. I was running from him. How would I kill him? I don't own a gun, sir."

"Yeah, I figured that. What about the town hall fire? Did you have a role in that?"

Jonah shook him off again.

"No sir. I have been hiding out at Dotsie's place. There is no way that I would leave there...it's too dangerous. I moved from the barn to the house where it was more safe, and I have not left...I swear."

After a few questions of lesser importance and a little small talk both men turned in for the night. Tom Johnson parked himself in the next cell with a shotgun at his side. Nobody was getting to the kid and the sheriff fell asleep knowing that tomorrow was going to be a very busy day.

Chapter Twenty Two

"Gee Albert, the movie was so good! By the way, thank you for the candy...that was sweet of you, get it? Sweet?"

Albert walked out of the movie theatre and onto the street with the swagger of a man who possessed immense wealth and importance. He looked to his left and noticed a few guys a year younger than him wishing they could be like him and have a girl as pretty as Margie. He was a wealthy man...wealthy in love.

"Sweet! I get it...how funny! You are sure swell, you know that? I guess I am one very lucky man."

Margie smiled and moved her body closer to his, almost burying herself in him as they walked slowly down the street to the soda fountain at the corner. He could smell her hair, her skin, her flowery perfumed scent as she nuzzled against him. Margie Reed was intoxicating.

The young lovers gazed into each other's eyes as they moved in unison and then the young lady spoke up with a soft giggle.

"What do you say we go on down to the park and spend some quality alone time together?"

Albert stopped suddenly and turned to her.

"Are you crazy? As much as I would love that...and believe me... I would definitely love that...your dad would kill me! We have to get home soon!"

"You worry too much. My dad is all bark and no bite...he's not going to kill you, especially since you take such good care of me and make me happy. He knows that we went to the movies and out for soda afterwards. Let's skip the soda shop and go down to the park."

Her devilish smile won him over instantly. He had wanted some time alone with her for a week and realized that tonight could be his lucky night.

"Let's go, but if we get caught it will be the end of both of us...I swear."

They took a turn at the corner and made their way down to the dark, quiet park. During the day this place of quiet refuge was a welcoming site but in the dark it had an ominous feel that left them both a little scared as well as excited. The couple sat down on a park bench and Margie went on the attack, a pleasant surprise for Albert.

After a minute of kissing, she pushed him farther with more passion in her actions. As she kissed his neck and lips she began to talk to him.

"I love bad boys." she whispered in a sultry voice.

"Are you a bad boy?"

More kissing.

"How bad are you? You ever commit a crime? You ever kill anyone?"

Albert stopped abruptly and leaned away with a look of panic on his face.

"What in the world did you just say? Have I ever KILLED anybody? Seriously? What the hell?"

"Oh come on, I'm just having fun. I'm sorry. But you know what? I really do get turned on by bad boys and something tells me you are REALLY bad."

They moved together and continued where they had left off. She was driving him insane with her sexuality and he lost all sense of who and where he was. She moaned and then whispered in his ear.

"You're so bad...what's the worst thing you have done. Tell me...tell me!"

She was panting and moving her hands all over him. He couldn't take it any longer and he muttered between kisses.

"I...killed...before. The fire at the town hall...that was me. Are you turned on?"

Margie leaned him down on the bench and crawled on top of him, continuing to make out with him. After a minute or two she became alarmed.

"We have to go now Albert! My dad will be looking for me...for us! We have been here too long. Don't worry Al, we will continue this...believe me we will continue this!"

The couple jumped up and straightened out their clothes in a heated panic, moving toward the edge of the park hastily. It was a hot, late summer night for the new lovers.

The outdoor front light of the house was on as the couple ran up the front lawn, stopping for a quick goodnight kiss before Margie ran into the house. Albert walked slowly back down the street to his house and, when the coast was clear Margie ran out the back door and out to her best friend's house.

A few more runs like this and I will be able to beat Jesse Owens in an Olympic race!

She ran up the front steps and pounded on the door, hoping she could roust her best friend. Dotsie peaked around the corner and down the stairs with nervous caution as she wondered who would be visiting after dark. Flipping on the outside light she recognized Margie right away and let her in.

"Dots, you're not going to believe this! You ARE NOT GOING TO BELIEVE THIS!"

"Believe what, Margie? Believe what?"

"I went to the movies with Albert, then talked him into making out with me at the park...very spooky by the way. Then as we were fooling around I got him to tell me all about it!"

"About what Mar...?"

Margie lowered her voice as if someone was listening in, an unconscious reflex.

"Albert told me that he burned the town hall and killed all those people!"

****

Dotsie found it impossible to sleep well, dozing off for a couple of minutes at a time. The news was too sensational to believe. Albert Crenshaw lit the town hall on fire and killed all those elders, including her dad and grandfather.

After a quick bath and brushing of her golden hair, she dressed and grabbed a piece of bread as she ran out of the house toward the middle of town. Dotsie hoped to catch the Sheriff and Jonah before there was too much activity at the jail.

"Let me see if I understand this...Albert confessed to your friend that he started the fire at the town hall?"

"Yes. Margie said he told her as they were kissing in the park."

"Kissing in the park? Why in the world would he tell her that he burned down the hall when they were getting romantic?"

"She made him tell her. She was turning him on and she asked about it. He told her he did it."

"You're serious...he blurted out that he killed people? That he started the fire? This seems a little too far-fetched, not to mention that she kind of coerced him into telling her what she wanted to hear. I don't think a judge or jury would buy any of this for a minute. We have no witnesses and a young boy who was led to say what your friend wanted to hear."

Dotsie's demeanor changed as she realized that what Albert said could mean very little.

"But you have to arrest him. I'm sure he started that fire and I think he may have killed Hunter."

"Killed Hunter? Really? Now we are set on charging him with murder as well as the arson and deaths of the town leaders? This is getting out of control. I cannot arrest a person based on suspicion with no tangible evidence. No court in the land is going to convict someone without real evidence, with only hearsay."

Dotsie knew she was defeated and stopped her pursuit for justice.

"Can I see Jonah now?"

The sheriff led her back to his cell where they could talk alone. She pulled up a wooden stool outside of the iron bars and they held hands.

"How are you? Are you all right? I miss you so much already."

A smile appeared on Jonah's face as he looked into her beautiful blue eyes.

"I miss you too…more than you know. Things are good here. I wish I was out at the house with you, but this is the safest place to be. Sheriff Tom believes that I am innocent and he is working to get the real killer. The food from the diner is delivered here and it's pretty good. I just worry that we may get overrun. The people were pretty crazy yesterday afternoon…they want to kill me."

The last phrase sent a shiver down Dotsie's spine and her eyes lowered with concern and fear.

"I know that Sheriff Tom will protect you." she muttered in a tone almost too quiet to hear.

Jonah looked into her eyes and reassured her that everything would be good. His bravado and positive outlook was needed to bring her spirits up.

"Don't worry Dots, he's going to figure it all out. Sheriff Tom is smart, and something tells me that he's already onto the fire starter. He will figure it out and I will be free to come home to you."

The way Jonah spoke his last words melted Dotsie's heart. *Come home to you...he's going to come home to me...to us.*

"Oh my god! I almost forgot to tell you!"

Dotsie then retold the story of Margie's date with Albert the night before and Jonah felt even more certain that his jail time would be coming to a quick end. Even with the disheartening news from Sheriff Tom it seemed evident that sooner or later Albert would be found out.

With a goodbye kiss through the jail cell bars, the couple vowed to be together soon and Dotsie reluctantly walked out of the jailhouse and back to the street. As she left through the large wooden doors a crowd was already starting to assemble with pleas to turn the prisoner over to them. With puzzled faces the mob began to realize that the young woman in front of them was on the side of the convict.

This is not good...this is really not good.

Chapter Twenty Three

Because neither Sheriff Tom or Jonah had much to do throughout the day, a fatigue descended on them, both mentally and physically. The dog days of summer in the Midwest had a way of making even the lazy seem over-exerted, moody, and tired. The temperature by midday had climbed over the one hundred degree mark and the protestors on their vigil outside the jailhouse temporarily gave up their quest for justice and hastily retreated to their abodes. The brightness of the sun made one's eyes hurt and their skin burn; a day like this was not welcome for many.

Night descended on the duo in the jail but it didn't bring much respite from the heat. The air was still and humidity oppressive as the two men settled in, one with a rifle by his side and the other secure behind bars. The open windows in the building offered no comfort and the small, metal desk fan also seemed to do little more than create a low humming noise. Both men drifted into a sweaty, uncomfortable slumber.

The noise came from somewhere in the distance, very far away from the depths of one's consciousness. The sheriff heard the thud and momentarily opened his eyes in the dark room, then fell back into his dream. Jonah never heard it, he never moved.

A dark, putrid smoke began to creep from the main area of the sheriff's office back to the holding cells and the acrid air stung Tom Johnson's nostrils. It set off an instant alarm to his system and he sat up suddenly with the realization that he was in the midst of trouble.

"Jonah! Jonah, wake up!"

The young man rolled over on his cot and his eyes opened widely in terror.

"We have to get out of here now!"

The smoke billowed under the three-panel door and up into their breathing space and fire began to roar in the next room.

"Follow me out the back of here! Quick!"

The sheriff unlocked Jonah's cell and both men scrambled for the exit at the end of the hall. A quick turn of his metal security key should have opened the door but it would not budge.

"Damn, it's blocked...someone blocked it!"

The fire grew quickly and the heat was building with an evil intensity. The creaking structure warned of its collapse.

"Get down low and follow me! We're going downstairs!"

The duo struggled back toward the main area of the building and the sheriff quickly opened a closet door that exposed dark, rickety wood stairs. The sheriff led the way down after flipping on a light switch that cast an eerie glow.

"Shut the door, hurry up!"

The fire raged overhead and they could hear a combination of falling objects and glass shattering. The hidden area they were contained in was a small space with an arsenal of weapons. Sheriff Tom grabbed a pistol and an old rifle and handed them to Jonah.

"We might need these...take them but don't use them until I tell you to. Consider yourself a deputy starting right now!"

Sheriff Tom then grabbed a revolver for himself and checked his rifle for ammunition. Both men had a box of bullets to go with their weapons and Tom led the way to the back corner of the room. An old, dust-covered door stood partially hidden along the brick wall and it was obvious that it hadn't been opened in a very long time.

"Bootleggers door, used to run booze...yeah, the last sheriff was in on it. Don't ask."

The door creaked open after some force and a dark tunnel lay ahead. Jonah peered in with curiosity and was hesitant to enter as he could see nothing beyond a few feet.

"Don't worry, follow me. It's safe...besides we can't stay here."

The men entered the cold, damp corridor and felt their way along a stone wall with their right hand. Jonah leaned as best as he could against the back of his leader with the fear of getting separated and lost.

"You alright?" the sheriff asked in a brave manner to mask his anxiety.

"Yeah, Tom...I'm fine. Where the hell does this go?"

"Just wait, you're in for a bit of a surprise. Mrs. Anderson told me about this."

A light chuckle from the sheriff broke up the seriousness of the moment. The corridor stopped at another wooden door and both men staggered into it, unable to see it until they hit it.

"We're here, we are safe."

The door opened into another basement and Tom found the switch to turn on the lights.

"Where are we?" Jonah asked as his pulse began to settle down.

They carefully climbed the stairs leading to a kitchen above and the sheriff called out to not alarm the inhabitants.

"Mrs. Rose? Mrs. Rose? Are you here?"

Carefully opening the basement door and peeking into the kitchen of the residence, Sheriff Tom called out again.

"Who's there?" a frightened old voice shrilled from another room.

"Mrs. Rose, its Sheriff Johnson...I'm in the kitchen."

The old lady appeared with an alarmed look and blurted out to her new guests.

"Oh my! Your office across the street is on fire! Did you know that, Sheriff?"

"Yes ma'am, we just escaped by using the tunnel."

"Oh yes, the tunnel." the old lady replied with a smile as she knew the reason her house was connected to the law center.

"That tunnel made me a small fortune! Why is your jail on fire?"

"Ma'am, I don't know. Someone was out to get us."

The sheriff moved to the side to let Jonah be acknowledged and the old lady gave an even broader smile.

"Well, well young man…you are quite the talk of the town here, aren't you?"

Jonah felt sheepish and didn't respond, he just nodded to the old lady.

The trio went to the front window of the parlor and looked across the street at the inferno taking place. The flames now climbed out of the roof and into the early morning sky, making the whole block a flickering image. It was evident that the building was well on its way to being a total loss.

A crowd gathered as it always does when an event of this magnitude hits a small town and now people were watching the fire department try to extinguish the blaze. Everyone knew they were fighting a lost cause, but fire is entertaining, and the crowd began to settle on Mrs. Rose' lawn as the morning sun began to bring on a new day.

"Sheriff, how did the fire start?"

"Mrs. Rose, we really don't know. One minute we were sound asleep and the next we were scrambling for our lives. Thank goodness we had the tunnel because someone blocked the back door. We would be dead without it. You didn't see anybody or anything suspicious, did you?"

The old lady frowned a bit and shook her head.

"I'm sorry, Sheriff. I didn't see a thing. The noise of the fire woke me up."

Jonah didn't say a word as he felt very guilty about the tragedy that was unfolding in front of him.

If it wasn't for me, the building would be fine and no one's life would be threatened. Those people in the township hall would be alive too.

Sheriff Johnson's eyes moved from the burning building to Jonah and back and he felt as if he could read the young man's mind.

"You know that you have nothing to do with this situation, right? The person or people who did this are sick. This isn't your fault, it's the fault of the crazies in town who have been doing bad things for a long time."

Jonah turned his look from the fire to the sheriff and old lady.

"If I hadn't shown up none of this would have happened."

Mrs. Rose spoke up before the sheriff could respond.

"Young man, this would have happened sooner or later. The people in this town are sick...you just had the courage or luck to escape with your life. That damned horrible tradition...manhood ritual...should have been stopped years ago. Most of the old coots who supported it are now dead from the township hall fire. This isn't about you, it's about an illness that the people of this town have harbored for a long time."

The sheriff nodded in agreement, relieved to know that he wasn't a part of the perverted rite of manhood. Then the old lady directed her attention to the lawman.

"Sheriff, there is something I need to talk to you about. Can I talk with you in the kitchen, alone?"

****

"Come on, Dennis, don't cry."

The big kid was hardly a teen and the first fire had scared him enough to slightly wet his pants. This fire was too much and he broke down in sobs as both the boys watched the plume of dark black smoke billow upward three blocks away.

"I don't want to do this anymore. I'm scared. We are going to die."

Albert moved back a step from his friend and showed a look of utter disbelief.

"Die? Are you kidding? We are just fine. I told you we would be just fine, right? Here we are and everything is fine!"

The big kid stopped his sobbing and dried his eyes with the back of his hand.

"Why do we have to keep making fires?"

Albert smiled and gave Dennis a reassuring look.

"This is the last one, ok? We won't do any more, I promise. You did really good today, right? I'm proud of you."

Dennis slowly smiled as his demeanor improved.

"You really mean that? I did good?"

"You did great buddy. Let's get away from here...let's go down by the park.

The next afternoon a couple walking along the creek near the beautiful expanse discovered the floating body of thirteen-year-old Dennis Reed.

Chapter Twenty Four

The sheriff's office was a total loss. The state fire marshal was brought in to assess the cause and monetary cost of the tragedy. Sheriff Johnson was thankful that he and his prisoner had escaped the blaze, but he was also furious with the realization that the townspeople could turn on him with such ferocity.

He set up his new office in the courthouse three blocks away, his space small and inadequate. The only good news he had been given was that insurance covered the loss of his old office and construction on a fancy, modern complex would commence immediately due to a special grant from the federal government's WPA. The sheriff hadn't seen the blueprints yet but was assured by government officials that it would be vastly superior to his old space. Chief Redding showed up with a pot of coffee and two cups from the town diner next door.

"You think that the government would build a new fire station for us as well as your jail?"

This hopeful suggestion from the new fire chief brought a chuckle from both the men as they shared early morning coffee.

"You know, that's not a bad idea. I will make sure to suggest it when I get a chance to sit down with the officials."

Chief Redding rolled his eyes toward the ceiling and let out a guffaw.

"We both know how the government bureaucracy works...fat chance."

The young sheriff offered a bit of hope to his new friend.

"With the WPA projects and all, your idea has a lot of merit. We just recently built a new county municipal building in Pierce and it has both fire and police combined. Your idea is pretty good and very practical. How old is the present station you have?"

"I think it was built when Abraham Lincoln was president!"

Both men laughed and Redding continued.

"I know that at one time it housed horses and water carriages. Remnants of the barn in the back are still there. I would guess that the assessment of Lincoln is pretty close...at least sixty years old."

Sheriff Johnson took a sip of his hot liquid, holding the cup with both hands as he leaned back slightly in his chair.

"This community has grown considerably since then. I say we propose it, it can't hurt to ask for it. On another note, what have you discovered from the jail fire?"

Redding took a sip of coffee and put his cup down on the desk.

"We both know it was arson. The big question is who set it. The doors were barricaded from the outside, it looks like the same iron used in the town hall fire. I'm guessing that the same person or people set you up to burn. They probably only wanted the kid, but I don't think it was a town posse...that would have attracted too much attention. I might be wrong though."

An early morning knock on the office door suddenly interrupted them.

"Come in." Sheriff Johnson invited, not being able to see who his guest was.

A tall, graying elderly man entered and there was a sudden sense deep inside the sheriff's mind that this visit was not a good one.

"Sheriff Johnson, I presume?" the guest inquired.

"Yes sir. What can I do for you?" the lawman responded while gesturing toward a seat for his guest.

The visitor moved slowly but deliberately toward the padded wooden chair and descended into it in a manner much too professional for your average run of the mill citizen. The fire chief excused himself and shut the office door behind him.

"Sheriff Johnson, let me introduce myself. My name is Tobias Richardson and I come to you from Washington. Washington D.C. that is."

Reaching into the breast pocket of his gray suitcoat he pulled out a standard mail sized envelope and handed it across the table. The sheriff looked at his guest and then the parcel.

"Go ahead and open it. It's an official notice from our agency concerning some events that have taken place in your community in the last month. Go ahead...open it up."

Johnson carefully tore open the seal and removed a folded piece of stationery. At the top was the government seal for the Federal Bureau of Investigation. His eyes moved across the lines and, as he expected, it was not good news.

"This comes from the top?" he inquired with dread.

"The very top. The United States Federal Bureau of Investigation has reason to believe that Jonah Edwards is an enemy of the state. We have information concerning the details of his probable murder of a man by the name of Hunter Carlyle. We also have witnesses who are prepared to testify that Jonah Edwards burned a township courthouse to the ground, killing twenty-five of the occupants...including the previous sheriff of this community. An additional bit of information was brought forth indicating that one Jonah Edwards is also responsible for burning your office and jail to the ground. Because the sheriff's office is technically government property, he is being indicted for a federal crime. That is why I am here today, to take Jonah Edwards into custody."

The sheriff sat in disbelief, not knowing how to respond. He sat back in his chair and took a moment to catch his breath and calm his mind before responding to the charges.

"Sir, first of all we have no evidence that points to Jonah Edwards committing the murder of Hunter Carlyle. There is none whatsoever. Secondly, we have no tangible evidence linking Mr. Edwards to the fire at the township hall...in fact we have a witness who can testify that he wasn't even present in town at the time of the fire.

Thirdly, he could not have set the fire at my office because he was in my jail and I was personally guarding him. We escaped together."

The lawman paused for a moment to let his comments sink in. Richardson's demeanor changed to one of confusion and the federal official shifted in his chair uncomfortably.

"Edwards was with you the whole time?"

"The whole time. I don't know who is feeding you this information in an effort to frame Mr. Edwards, but the charges that you have brought here are wildly inaccurate. You're pursuing the wrong person."

Richardson sat back and studied the sheriff quietly, not knowing whether to believe him or not.

"Sheriff, can you explain to me why Mr. Edwards was in your custody when the fire broke out?"

Tom Johnson relaxed slightly as he hoped his explanation would clear everything up.

"I took Jonah Edwards into custody to save him. The townspeople suspected that he was the killer and arsonist, and they organized a posse to get rid of him, to execute him. I figured out where he was staying and I jailed him to protect him. We were fine until the fire."

Richardson's eyes narrowed as he glared across the desk at Johnson.

"And where is Mr. Edwards now?"

An uncomfortable silence hung over both men, one that seemed to last forever.

"I am not at liberty to expose his whereabouts."

"What do you mean...not at liberty? He is wanted on a federal warrant which means you have to take him into custody yourself or give us his whereabouts."

"If I give him up the townspeople will kill him, or worse you will convict him and give him the death penalty. I know for a fact that he is not guilty of at least two of your charges."

"Sheriff Johnson…what charge is he possibly guilty of? Which one?"

Johnson paused again, not wanting to incriminate the young man.

"The only charge I cannot refute is the one on Hunter Carlyle. The other charges will never stick."

"But the charge on the death of Carlyle could be accurate and is worth pursuing. He could very well have at a minimum committed manslaughter, maybe murder. On that charge alone we need to take Mr. Edwards into custody. Where is he?"

The fear in his mind now being realized, the sheriff was ready to make a deal with the federal agent.

"I'm not going to disclose his location, but I will take him into custody for you. I need your assurance that he will get a proper lawyer and a fair trial. Can I count on you for that?"

The federal agent relaxed in stature and nodded in agreement.

"Of course. You take him into custody. We will try him. He will get a proper lawyer, one that you can provide or we will provide if necessary. We will hold the trial in this locale, your jurisdiction. But you need to bring him in, failure to do so will result in your contempt of our federal justice system. We will take your badge."

Johnson stood up and reached across the table to shake hands on the deal with Richardson.

"You have twenty-four hours to take Jonah Edwards into custody...twenty-four hours from right now."

Chapter Twenty Five

"Jonah, don't go! You can't go! They will convict you for sure, these people are crazy and they just want someone to hang for Hunter's death!"

Sheriff Johnson stood silent on the front steps of Dotsie's house, his duty repulsive to his sense of justice.

"Jonah, I must take you in. I have no choice; the feds are pressing me. I have less than a day to take you in before they come for you. If they have to pursue you it's going to be bad...it will look like you are evading federal marshals. They will put you on the most wanted list if you run and you will not have a chance against them."

Jonah stood inside the doorway with his head down, fighting the urge to both cry and run. Tears started to run down Dotsie's face as she could no longer be strong. To both of them the end felt certain and near.

"Why can't I just stay here? This is working just fine."

Johnson looked from Jonah to Dotsie and back again.

"The only reason you are safe here since the fire is because everyone thinks you are living with me under house arrest. They fear the gun. It's just a matter of time before they figure out that you are back here again and then they will get you. Taking you into federal custody is the safest thing for all of us."

Jonah's head dropped and he kicked gently at the floor. Dotsie fell into him and held him tightly, not wanting him to go.

"Jonah, I will get you the best lawyer in the land. The charges being brought forth will never stick, regardless of who tries to prosecute this case. Two of the three charges against you have already been reputed and the third one has no evidence. Come with me now and I will keep you in custody like before. You will be safe, and this will all be over before you know it. You will be a free man."

"Safe? Safe? You are joking, right? We were damned nears burned to death by the townspeople the last time you told me we were safe! There is no such thing as safe and there are no guarantees that these people will not convict and hang me. There is no such thing as safe."

The sheriff could understand Jonah's viewpoint and he nodded in agreement with the young man. He had to convince him that this time was different.

"This situation...this lockup is different. We have federal marshals on their way to protect both of us. The townspeople will be intimidated, put in their place. They are not going to take on the federal police the way they stood up to us. You need to trust me on this. Soon this will all be over and you will be free."

Jonah shifted his gaze between his girlfriend and the lawman and finally consented as he held Dotsie in a tender embrace. She began to sob uncontrollably, and he did everything he could to console her and tell her that it would all be over soon.

He pulled away after a kiss, walked out the front door, and down the porch stairs to the waiting squad car. Jonah sat down in the back seat, more scared than he had ever been in his life. Sheriff Tom looked over and nodded to him with reassurance.

"You need to trust me on this, Jonah. This will all be over and you will be back here for good."

The car slowly pulled onto the road back to town and Dotsie collapsed in a teary puddle on her living room sofa. After a good cry she composed herself and prayed to the heavens with all her might.

Please bring him back, Lord, please keep him safe.

The police car pulled up to the front of the courthouse and two federal agents in dark suits were waiting along with Richardson. A sense of relief came over the agents and they quietly led Jonah inside the building.

The process of taking Jonah into custody was very casual as both Richardson and

Tom Johnson wanted to keep the young man as calm and comfortable as possible. The intense gravity of the situation had lightened considerably since the first meeting between the two lawmen. The federal agent now realized that there was less substance to the claims against Jonah Edwards than there appeared to be a day earlier, when he set out to bring the young man to justice.

While being very diligent in his duties, Tobias Richardson had also come to the realization that he might have been played as a fool by the people in this isolated town. Everything seemed to be just a formality now and while Jonah was not out of danger of prosecution, he was certainly safer than he had been in the past.

The district judge would be making his rounds and would be in town for the trial in a week and a half. Time seemed to drag on forever in Jonah and Dotsie's world. Daily visits began to take on an air of doom and the only thing that lifted the young couple's spirits was the reassurance that Tom Johnson kept preaching.

"Soon this will all be over and everything will be back to normal."

Chapter Twenty Six

The morning sun sprayed down upon the bricks and cement that decorated the historic downtown area. The bright rays of light created an unconventional heat wave in the middle of autumn. Everyone was moving slower than normal, methodically, almost caught off guard with this newborn summer of sorts.

All the citizens turned their attention to the massive brick courthouse on the north side of the town square, a building designed to give off the unmistakable air of supreme importance. This grandiose, dark structure would be the venue of the biggest court case to hit the small town in over a half century. The daily nine o'clock ringing of the chimes in the center tower would signal the start of the proceedings and everyone understood that the gallery would be full at least an hour before.

The honorable John J. Clark would be running the show. A long-standing judge in this area, it was well known that he would rule with an iron fist. The most powerful man in the Midwest moved with careful grace to the bench. His small, elderly frame, topped with thinning gray hair and outlined in an oversized black robe gave the impression of frailty. His look was indeed deceptive, as he was tougher than a junkyard dog.

The bailiff announced the judge as he entered the courtroom from a side door and, in an irate mood, Clark directed everyone to be seated. Jonah glanced quickly toward Dotsie and the look of silent dread made her heart drop. The only hope lay in the fact that the defense attorney, Edgar Rice, would save her man's life. Burning the meeting house and killing the men inside surely meant the death penalty if convicted.

The prosecution started the trial after a quick announcement of the case and rules of conduct by Judge Clark. The prosecuting attorney was Morris Williams, a distant uncle to Hunter Carlyle. Dressed in his Sunday best, the large, middle-aged man had the look of a shark about to attack its prey. He glared at Jonah, then Dotsie, then the jury and everyone seemed to give off a shiver of fear.

Williams gave his initial address, and it was immediately obvious that he was going to do everything in his power to convict the boy who killed many of his closest friends by burning them alive. His description of the crime in his opening statement was graphic and grotesque, meant to shake up everyone in the hot, airless room.

Both attorneys sparred verbally in an elaborate dance designed to gain their advantage in the case and after two hours of back-and-forth argument the judge called a recess for lunch. Jonah rose weakly and almost fainted. In his mind, the case was already decided and he would be hanging in the center of the town within days. Having no appetite, he asked to be returned directly to his cell in the basement. The young defendant nodded slowly to his lover and then was escorted away from the scene.

Dotsie walked towards the back of the full gallery, waiting patiently as each row of gawkers dispersed to the double doors at the rear. Suddenly Albert appeared at her side, a satisfied look upon his face.

"What do you think, Dots?" he whispered with a little too much glee in his voice.

"What do you mean by what do you think?"

She stopped in her tracks and faced him directly with a scowl. The little man was taken aback with her demeanor.

"I'm just curious as to what you think...no big deal."

"We both know he is innocent. He's being framed by someone and it's not fair."

Her face showed her pain and helplessness. Albert struggled to find words to provide her with comfort as he was enjoying the spectacle.

"I don't know about innocent, but I know that life is not always fair."

His words hung in mid-air, and she stepped back in a stunned manner.

"We both know he is innocent, Albert. We both know."

The comment wasn't meant to be antagonistic, and he reached out to put his arm around the damsel in distress. She flashed a stunned look that screamed out 'are you kidding?' and pushed him away, quickly exiting to the hallway. The little man did not attempt to follow as he knew nothing could help her now. He would become her knight in shining armor after Jonah hung from the rope.

The hour break passed much too quickly and as people re-entered the courtroom the heat hit them like a wave. Sweat poured freely from all and the air took on a lived-in odor. Jonah was escorted back to his chair at the front and the battle between the two assertive men and the judge began anew.

By two o'clock no one could stand the heat any longer and Judge Clark seemed to be affected the most. With the constant dabbing of his brow and slow, struggled breathing, he dismissed everyone for the day as no one seemed to have the upper hand in the life-dependent argument.

Jonah's attorney was well known as the most fair and intelligent man in the state, possibly even the Midwest. He descended the steep stairway to the basement where Jonah was being held and he pulled up a wooden stool at the front of the jail cell to go over the day's events with his client.

"Well young man, how are you doing after today's circus?"

Jonah was in no mood for small talk. He shrugged and frowned as he sat on his cot with his back against the cool brick wall of his cell.

"I think you should know that we have a very good chance of winning this case. We don't have to make any kind of bargain here; we will just win it outright. Don't worry, kid. You will be back home before you know it. This isn't my first rodeo and I have a few tricks up my sleeve."

"I have overheard some people here saying that if I am found guilty they are going to hang me in the town square. Is this true?"

The wise old attorney shook his head and laughed softly.

"Jonah, most of the people in this town have no idea of what the hell they are talking about. They are so backwards here...they are living in a time of the wild west fifty years or more ago. You are being tried in a federal court and so the federal system will carry out your sentence. At worst you will end up doing your prison time at Leavenworth, down south from here. They could give you the death penalty, but it isn't going to happen. We are going to win this case because I always win."

Jonah produced a quiet smile as he took in the hopeful arrogance of the gentleman he hoped would save him.

"Mr. Rice, how many cases have you won? How many cases like mine?"

The defense attorney let out a chuckle and a wide smile. He unfolded his large hands from the front of his torso and pointed at Jonah with vigor.

"Young man, I always win. Don't you worry, I ALWAYS WIN."

****

Another scorching day beat down upon the small, midwestern town and the citizens felt compelled to watch the demise of the young man that many were now referring to as 'the Devil Kid'. No one could foresee what the day would bring, but there was an unusual anticipation in the air.

Most assumed that today would be the day that the verdict would be brought down upon the guilty subject and the young man would be sentenced to hang for his vicious crime. Some of the townsmen were already figuring out how to properly build a sturdy hangman's scaffold in the town square. Lumber was being donated by the local mill for the cause.

Judge Clark called the court to session and Edgar Rice immediately shocked everyone in the crowded room with a demand to approach the bar. Both lawyers walked to the front and spoke in whispers with the old judge. After a minute of dialogue, the spectators in the courtroom couldn't help but notice the agitation on the face of Morris Williams.

"I will not stand for this...this is absolutely preposterous!" he blurted out to the quiet court.

"I will direct you to keep your tone low, do you understand?"

Judge Clark barked loud enough to scare even the hardest men and women in the gallery. The sudden scolding by the judge silenced the old prosecutor and he looked suddenly defeated.

Edgar Rice turned toward his client and the gallery and jurors saw a smile creep across his face. His expression gave away the fact that a surprise was on its way. Both men returned to their tables and Williams sat down with exaggerated force in his chair.

Rice remained standing and whispered to Jonah.

"Watch this, kid."

The people in the gallery overheard the old attorney and a buzz quickly moved through the spectators. Judge Clark brought his gavel down hard on his desk a half a dozen times and shouted out to the room.

"Order in the court! Order in the court, damn it! There will be order in my court, do you understand?!"

The room was startled and quieted quickly, as no one wanted to cross the grumpy old man. The commotion went instantly silent.

"You will all behave in my court or you will all be thrown out. I can try this case in an empty courtroom if I need to, and I will do it. Do you understand?"

No one said a word, everyone just nodded sheepishly. Order was restored.

"Mr. Rice, the floor is yours for your next witness."

Everyone turned to Rice, the only person standing in the room.

"Your honor, the defense would politely request permission to call Mrs. Ivory Rose to the stand."

The gasp that followed this request was loud enough to wake the dead and the judge scowled while raising his gavel above his head. He didn't have to bring it down; everyone quieted in an instant.

"The court requests the presence of Mrs. Ivory Rose. Is Mrs. Rose present?" Clark yelled out to the audience.

Everyone turned to their neighbors to locate the old lady. Nobody found success in their search. Then the large, oak double doors at the back of the room opened and Sheriff Johnson escorted the elderly woman into the venue. He held her arm gently and guided her to the stand. It was pretty apparent that she could get to the front under her own power, but she seemed to enjoy the company of the young, handsome law officer.

A grin filled her face as she looked at the onlookers on her way to the front of the courtroom, nodding to a few of her closer acquaintances. Sitting on the stand, she turned to smile at Judge Clark and his demeanor instantly changed.

The old man was visibly charmed by the fancy, elderly woman and she could have demanded almost anything of him at that moment. Eyes locked knowingly around the room and everyone was surprised by the sudden sense of affection between the judge and woman called to testify. Dotsie shared a tender smile with Jonah.

Edgar Rice slowly approached the stand with a professional sense of authority and began by affirming the old lady's identity with a bit of small talk. She warmed up to his joviality. Then the key questions began.

"Mrs. Rose, is it true that you live at 124 Liberty Street? Right here in the middle of town?"

"Yes, sir. Been here almost all my life. My husband died ten years ago; you know? Still live in my house though."

She shot Judge Clark a gently smile and glance and he returned a compassionate gaze.

"Do you recall where you were on the night of July 7th of this summer?"

She turned to the jury and confidently gave her response.

"Why yes. I was where I am pretty much every night during the summer. I was just sitting on my front porch, knitting a baby blanket for Sarah Smith. It was a beautiful little blanket...she had a little girl you know, prettiest little thing I ever seen. She has her mother's eyes, the little doll."

Ivory Rose turned to check Judge Clark's response and was pleasantly surprised at how attentive he was. Edgar Rice did his best to steer her back to her testimony.

"I'm sure she is, Mrs. Rose. If you please, I have another question for you."

Rice turned toward the jury and gave them a confident smile. He looked quickly at Jonah, smiled again, and then turned back to the witness stand.

"Did you happen to see anything unusual on that night? Anything at all out of the ordinary?"

One could have cut the silence with a knife as everybody was on edge.

"Yes. I saw two young men sneaking across the street. A smaller one was in the lead with a bigger person behind carrying a container and sticks toward the old town hall. They were moving very quickly...I'm sure they didn't see me as it was getting dark. Then a couple of minutes later they ran right by me, right down the sidewalk in front of my house. Pretty soon I could see the smoke and flames on the other side of the square and all hell broke loose. Pardon my language, Judge."

The old lady flashed a pretty grin toward the bench and the judge nodded with a tender smile.

"It all happened so quickly. Then one of them walked back toward the fire. This was very strange."

"Mrs. Rose, can you identify the young men you saw so clearly?"

"Yes sir, I know one of them. I've known him for years. Albert Crenshaw."

The room exploded in sound as everyone turned to identify the newly accused. As they pivoted toward the gallery all they saw were the tall double doors closing back upon them. Whoever was standing in the back had now exited quickly and it took a moment before the crowd of onlookers realized what had happened.

Judge Clark rose with fury and yelled out to his lawmen in the room.

"Get Albert Crenshaw now!"

Chapter Twenty Seven

With the courtroom in deafening chaos, the judge called for immediate recess and the bailiff allowed a minute for Dotsie to talk to Jonah before leading him back to jail. Edgar Rice also made sure to give the two young people a moment to embrace and kiss before he gave reassurance to both that everything would be alright. Jonah was then led back downstairs to his cell.

Dotsie didn't want to participate in any hunt and chase of Albert Crenshaw. Her hatred of him came from the deepest depth of her heart. In her mind he was the reason that everything between her and Jonah was taken away and Jonah's life was now in danger. With solemn resolution, Dotsie vowed to kill Albert herself if she ever got her hands on him.

Edgar Rice paid his client a quick visit in the basement of the courthouse and wore a grin as he sat down on a small stool outside of the iron cell bars.

"Quite a day upstairs, huh?" he chuckled as his voice gave off a hollow echo in the corridor.

"You knew exactly what you were doing up there, didn't you?" Jonah whispered quietly with an equal smile.

"I did my homework. I talked to everyone in this little burg. People see things, people talk. All you need to do is find the person that was in the right place at the right time. Ivory Rose was that person. Often it is the little old lady that sits alone, soaking up everything around her. I looked at the crime scene, then the main street, and then looked for the little old lady. She was the second person I interviewed."

Jonah felt a sense of confidence and relief come over him.

This might all work out.

"Mr. Rice? When will I be able to get out of here?"

The wise attorney understood his client's impatience and despair.

"We have a bit of a ways to go yet. You will be cleared of the township hall and there are no charges anymore concerning the jail fire, but the Carlyle case still poses a bit of a challenge. I'm afraid that you might be here a bit longer, but hang on to hope, kid. I am doing my homework and I will get you out of this. I ALWAYS DO MY HOMEWORK. ALWAYS!"

The smile faded from Jonah's face as he pondered his predicament.

"Are the townspeople going to hang me?" he asked with a timid tone, fearing the response from Rice.

"Goodness no." the experienced attorney replied with conviction.

"That's a bunch of hooey. Unless they stormed the jail and took you hostage themselves it will never happen. This is a case under federal jurisdiction and so the townspeople, county, and state have no right to convict anyone and appropriate punishment. Besides, Albert Crenshaw is the target of this town now. You are no longer Public Enemy Number One. The citizens here are now combing the area, high and low, for Albert."

"Do you think that Albert burned down the township hall...that he killed all those people?"

The seasoned lawyer gave his client a look of doubt and a shrug.

"I don't know, Jonah. It is believed that a person is innocent until proven guilty. The eyewitness account by Mrs. Rose certainly doesn't help Albert's cause. Why would he do such a thing? We would have to establish a motive, a reason for his actions. How reliable is Mrs. Rose? That's another question to consider. Personally, I think she is very reliable. Judging by what just happened upstairs, I think she just gained a large amount of credibility with the judge and jury. Albert basically convicted himself and added to her credibility by making a run for it. It will be up to the court system to bring formal charges and try him for the crime."

Jonah nodded in understanding as he sat on his cot with his knees pulled up to his chest.

"I can tell you this, though. I think you are off the hook, so to speak. The prosecutor has no evidence linking you to the townhall fire. You also have a solid alibi. We can call Dotsie up to the stand if we need. Honestly, I believe that these charges should have never been brought upon you."

"I don't want to involve Dotsie in any of this." Jonah declared with conviction.

"We probably won't have to. I am guessing that the old judge will throw the charges out. With no credible evidence in the murder of Hunter Carlyle he will dismiss that case as well. It might cause a bit of a problem with the townspeople...they are out for blood, you know? But I'm sure we can find a way to fix all of this and have you out of here soon. Just hang in there."

Edgar Rice had more work to complete and he went on his way, leaving Jonah to feel more confident than he had been in a very long time.

Things could be a whole lot worse. I'm safe down here, the food is pretty good, and it's much cooler here than up on the street. Temperature could climb over one hundred degrees...not a bad time to be here. I miss Dots though...so much. I wish she was here with me.

No sooner did he make his wish than she appeared, a stunning, youthful vision of beauty strolling toward him in her light summer dress while carrying a small, white box in her hands.

"Look what I've got. A special treat for us."

She opened the box to reveal a thick square of chocolate fudge and Jonah couldn't help but smile widely.

"Where did you get that? Will they even allow that in here?"

Dotsie laughed at his questions in a way that made him love her more.

"Sheriff Tom is fine with this. He thought it was cute when I talked to him upstairs. He's on our side, you know? Anyways, I ran across the street to Olson's Candy Shop...the old man makes the best fudge.

Thought you'd like some and we could celebrate your freedom."

"Dotsie, I am not free yet."

Jonah grabbed the bars in front of him with both hands for emphasis.

"Not yet, but you will be. Both Mr. Rice and Sheriff Tom think so. You will be out of here before you know it."

The young prisoner let go of the bars and leaned his chest against them, enjoying the coolness through his shirt. Dotsie broke off a messy chunk of fudge and handed it to him with a giggle, her hands now a mess. Taking a piece herself, they both savored the chocolate goodness.

The quiet, shared moment between lovers was suddenly interrupted by an opened door and the echo of footsteps signaling Edgar Rice's return.

"Good news, Jonah. Very, very good news! Judge Clark wants to meet with us at three o'clock in his chamber. He has called Morris Williams to the meeting as well. I think he's going to dismiss the charges and set you free."

This news brought a squeal of delight from Dotsie and a proud smile from Jonah.

"We are not totally in the clear yet. It may be dangerous to have you released back into the public. The sheriff is worried about your safety...the townspeople may not agree with what Judge Clark might do. I'd be lying if I told you that I am not worried either. Some of these people are crazy, they don't respect the law. They still feel that vengeance for the murder of Hunter is necessary."

"I might have to stay here?" Jonah asked in sudden disbelief.

"Not necessarily. We will have to see what happens at three 'o clock... we will know where we stand and what we can do after that. Keep your hopes up, both of you. This will all work out in the end."

With that gentle reassurance, the attorney pivoted toward the door at the end of the corridor and exited with self- confidence.

"It's going to be fine, Dots. He's good. I'll be out before the sun sets."

****

Albert Crenshaw never expected this sudden change in events. The panicked young man moved quickly with fear and was surprisingly more alert than he had ever been in his life. He knew exactly where to go, was not going to be caught, and if apprehended could talk his way out of trouble, something he had so many times throughout his life. Albert Crenshaw knew with genuine certainty that he would not be taken down.

True to his conviction, none of the rabid townspeople could locate the newest fugitive. Everyone searched with a fervor, looking in every possible place and yet nobody could find the runaway. A dire puzzlement enveloped the town as people were now befuddled as to what had happened hours earlier in the courtroom.

Was Jonah Edwards innocent? It couldn't be true. He was the killer, the devil boy. Albert Crenshaw? One of their own, their kin? Devious and smarmy yes, but a killer? It couldn't be. The killer had to be the devil boy...this was some kind of trick by that fancy lawyer that rolled into town so boldly. Never trust an outsider...whether criminal or lawyer...was there a difference?

Chapter Twenty Eight

After spending another hour together talking about their feelings for each other and their future, Dotsie made her way home to prepare their house for Jonah's arrival. Excitement ran through her whole being as she walked lightly down the gravel road to her farm on the outskirts of the town.

The sun shone with an uncommon intensity but she didn't mind the extreme heat. The humidity that would normally bother her on a day like this seemed non-existent. Dotsie felt like she was walking on air; not a care in the world. She really believed what Mr. Rice told her, what Sheriff Tom told her, and most importantly what Jonah told her. *Jonah loves me. Jonah Edwards loves me. Mrs. Jonah Edwards.*

Three o'clock seemed to take a lifetime to arrive and when the bells rang out in the town square with a trio of loud chimes, Jonah was ready to head upstairs. Edgar Rice and Sheriff Tom appeared on the second-floor landing and the trio moved to Judge Clark's chamber.

The sheriff opened the ornate wooden door and allowed the attorney and his subject to enter. An overhead fan provided the only breeze in the room, its whirring a welcome distraction, and while the air was hot at least it wasn't stuffy.

The judge sat behind a desk that made him look both small and yet important at the same time, a contradiction that brought a smile to Jonah's face. Morris Williams stood on one side of the room with a scowl that gave the impression that he had soiled himself. Jonah felt the temptation to chuckle but held it back. His frayed nerves seemed to make everything humorous.

Judge Clark rose and gestured to three open chairs on the left.

"Please take a seat, gentlemen."

After the trio was settled in the stately antique armchairs, the judge began the meeting.

"As we all recognize, the events of earlier today have shed an unexpected, entirely new light on our proceedings. Even though we do not know to what extent Mr. Albert Crenshaw is involved in any of this case, we do know that the charges brought by the prosecution now seem very weak."

Clark paused for effect and glared toward Morris Williams. The prosecutor didn't dare say a word as he knew he would bring hellfire from the old judge.

"Quite frankly, despite witness testimony given to the federal officers I feel that there is little credible evidence available to hold Mr. Edwards...there is no legal reason to detain or incarcerate this young man."

The judge now gestured toward Jonah and a small, compassionate smile crossed his wrinkled complexion.

"I have taken many hours over the last two days to review the charges, the eyewitness accounts, and all the other circumstances regarding all three counts brought before my court. Quite frankly, if the federal courts had not assigned me to this mess, I would have thrown it out before it ever reached this stage in our legal process. A large part of the information submitted for this trial seems to be pure hogwash."

Morris Williams recoiled with a bit of hesitation and fear at the old man's bold language and Edgar Rice smiled and nodded in agreement. He snuck a sideways glance at Jonah and saw a smile form across the defendant's face.

"I have a much larger concern at hand. I am concerned about the safety of Jonah Edwards after he is released from custody. The townspeople will not be happy with what I am about to do. I will ask that the prosecuting attorney, Mr. Williams, make a public statement that is strong enough... convincing enough, to convey a message that the people of this town are to no longer bother Mr. Edwards."

"But your honor, I cannot just come out and declare Mr. Edwards innocent of all the charges against him. We have not finished the court proceedings, the judicial process. The people of this town will hang me!"

The prosecutor's face showed a mixture of terror and disbelief as he knew his fate was dire. The judge gave him a look that would have frozen the heartiest of souls.

"Mr. Williams! Allow me to make myself clear here. I do not think you understood what I just said. You will be meeting with a newspaper man who may be sitting out there in the waiting room as we speak. You will clear Jonah Edwards of all the charges against him and you will do it in a manner that ensures his safety. I absolutely do not care what the hell you say to that newsman, but it had better be good...damn good. If you fail in your attempt to save this young man, I will see to it that you will never, and I mean NEVER, practice law anywhere again. Not even in Tahiti! Do you understand me, Counselor?"

The prosecutor, visibly shaken, sank in his chair, his shoulders drooped forward. His high-profile case was now lost, and the townspeople could probably make him the new target of their bloodthirsty anger. He nodded meekly to the judge.

"Sheriff Johnson, please see to it that you do your best to protect Mr. Williams. Make whatever statement is necessary to deflect any and all blame from the prosecutor. I want the townspeople to realize that this decision is no reflection on Mr. Williams. Aside from accompanying him around town or guarding him while he is here, try to make sure he is safe."

"Yes sir, your honor."

"Now, for our next item of business. The protection for Mr. Jonah Edwards. Young man, you will be released from custody when we leave this room. I am going to attach a stipulation to your freedom, however. You will be ordered by the court to stay in informal custody with Sheriff Johnson. He will house you for the period of one week while we continue to straighten this whole situation out. When the sheriff is at work, you will be at work as well, housed right here in the government center. When he goes home you are to go with him. You will not leave his side when he is off duty. We will meet back here one week from today, same time, to evaluate your safety and permanent release."

Jonah had expected to walk free from the courthouse and now it sounded to him like he was still incarcerated, just in a different place. His heart dropped as he wondered how he could explain this to Dotsie. The judge noticed the change in his demeanor instantly.

"Young man, you don't need to worry. This arrangement is temporary. I have every reason to believe that in a week from now you will be free to go on with your life. I am just making the provision to guarantee your safety until then. Keep your chin up, you have done well."

The judge stood up, straightened his tie and dabbed sweat from his forehead, and gave a nod of approval and encouragement to Jonah. Then he turned his attention back to Morris Williams.

"We are now dismissed. Mr. Williams, you know what you need to do...don't screw this up."

The judge then acknowledged Sheriff Tom and nodded, shifting his beady eyes back and forth between Williams and the law enforcement officer.

Jonah was temporarily placed back in his basement jail cell while the sheriff climbed back upstairs to face the news reporter who was in the process of grilling Morris Williams. Half an hour later Sheriff Tom returned to Jonah.

"Ready to go? Do not do anything crazy, just stick by me. Who knows, maybe I will deputize you and give you a badge."

Both men shared a quiet laugh and a smile as they moved upstairs and out into the free world.

Chapter Twenty Nine

Something in the deepest part of his mind rousted him awake in the dark room. The fog that accompanies the brain when waking up too quick vanished as he knew he had to check on the house and more importantly, on the kid in the next room.

Rolling over slowly, he turned on his bedside lamp and surveyed the room. The same perpetual mess of boots, trousers, and once worn shirts lay in heaps like obstacles that he would have to avoid if he were to reach the door to the room.

Sheriff Tom stepped out into the cold, dark hallway and moved with caution to the smaller bedroom on his right. Opening the door carefully so as not to wake his guest, he let out an expletive when he saw the vacant bed.

"Damn it, kid! Where are you? No! Jonah? Jonah?"

The lawman's voice raised in volume with each call of the young man's name and both panic and frustration flooded the sheriff's mind. With no response coming from within the house, Tom moved quickly from the bedroom to the bathroom, down the steps, and through the rest of the dwelling. Jonah was nowhere to be found.

"Damn it, I knew I couldn't trust him!"

Frustration became rage as he bolted back up the stairs two at a time. Entering the mess of his room, he grabbed the first pair of his uniform pants and shirt that he could locate and then he located his holstered weapon on the bedside table. The lawman knew exactly where to find his escapee.

****

Getting from the rented farmhouse to the middle of town was the hardest part of the process for Jonah and he cursed silently to himself that he had not paid enough attention to the route that Sheriff Tom had used earlier in the day.

As he reached the center of town his pace picked up to a light jog while he kept an eye out for anyone following him. Jonah's disposition was brightening as he moved closer to his destination.

Midnight had yet to descend on the Gravelle farmstead and Dotsie was already enjoying a sleepover with her best friend. With the radio playing music quietly and a bowl of popcorn shared between them, Margie and Dotsie sat on the worn, old sofa and talked about what had happened at the courthouse over the last couple of days.

A sharp knock on the front door startled them and halted their words as they faced each other with puzzled expressions. Dotsie rose from her seat and moved over to the radio, turning it off with a quick flip of the switch on the front.

"Wait here. I don't know who this could be, but it might be Jonah!"

Dotsie moved with excitement to the door and opened it quickly, only to find Albert standing on the front steps with a hopeful grin.

"Albert?! What are you doing here? It's almost midnight!"

The look on the young woman's face and harshness in her words cut into his spirit as he immediately perceived a non-welcome feeling.

"I came out to check on you, Dotsie. I was worried about you and thought that maybe I could provide you some company."

His explanation sent a chill up and down her spine.

What does he mean by company?

"Hey Dots, who's there?" Margie called from the parlor.

"Margie? Margie is here?" Albert asked with surprise and disappointment.

"Yes, and we are fine. You can go on your way...thank you very much."

The visitor's smile turned dark instantly as he pushed his way over the threshold and into the small entryway.

"Dotsie, I am here to protect you. I won't be going anywhere."

Margie stepped around the corner of the wall and picked up the cold tension between her friend and the boy who she thought had fallen for her.

"Hello, Margie. Fancy finding you here. You told someone about our date and our little discussion, didn't you?"

Now Margie felt fear fall upon her as she slowly backed up into the parlor as if being pushed by Albert. He moved to the center of the room and scanned the area for any more people, in particular for Jonah.

"So Dotsie...where is Jonah? I figured that I would find him here, that is if you two are still a couple? You know you could be so happy with me. Think about it, just the two of us. We could live here and be the most prominent couple in town...we could run this place, you and me."

"You two?" Margie blurted with shock.

"Shut up, Margie. You talk too much... maybe you should go now and leave us alone."

"Don't tell her to shut up! She's not going anywhere, Albert. She's my best friend, my guest, and she is staying here with me."

The smitten young man felt his plans unravel before him because he hadn't anticipated that anyone would be at the farm except for Dotsie and possibly Jonah. He was gambling on the chance to get rid of the devil boy and court the young lady.

Albert impulsively pulled the revolver that once belonged to Dotsie's father from his waist band and held it at his side, making sure both girls saw it.

"Sit down now."

"Albert, what the..."

"I said sit down now."

Dotsie and Margie looked at the gun, Albert's face, and then at each other as they backed up toward the sofa and carefully sat down next to each other.

"There you go. That's not so bad, is it? Margie, I bet you wished you had left when I told you to. This would have been so much easier."

He sat across from them on an ornate armchair that hadn't been used since Dotsie's mom was alive. With a smug look, Albert casually waived the pistol around as he started to ramble on.

"Dots...you and me. We would be SO GOOD together. You could have it all, I could give you everything you want in life. You see, I am going places...I am going to be somebody. Heck, I will probably be the mayor here someday, or maybe even more. You don't really want Jonah...you don't need Jonah. Sooner or later he will be back in jail and, even if he's not, he will never be as successful as me. You and me, Dotsie, you and me."

The pistol had struck fear in both the women, but now that Dotsie realized that she was the center of attention it made her sick to her stomach. She couldn't find any words to speak, nothing to say that might keep her from getting shot. Suddenly she had an idea.

"You know, Al, you are right. I guess I didn't know how much you cared for me, cared about me, and I am flattered. I thought you liked Margie...all along it was me?"

"It has always been you, Dotsie."

"Margie, you should go now. I will be fine; Albert is here with me."

Margie's eyes grew wide as she looked with bewilderment at her best friend and then slowly rose from the sofa toward the door. Albert didn't budge and the pistol was lowered onto his lap.

Margie quietly closed the front door behind her and then ran with all the speed she could muster toward town. Tears started to stream down her face, making it hard for her to see in the dark as she moved down the dirt road.

"Margie! What are you doing here?"

Jonah was running toward the farmstead and Margie ran to him and hugged him hard.

"What's wrong, Margie? What's wrong?"

Chapter Thirty

The duo approached the moonlit yard and farmhouse as quietly as they could with Margie whispering to Jonah.

"They were in the front parlor. Albert is facing away from the window so hopefully we can see what is going on."

"Stay back, stay behind me. We can't afford to get caught, especially if he has a gun."

Jonah moved toward the rustic double window at the front of the house and rose up to peer inside. With the window slightly ajar, he could hear through the screen and what he heard surprised him.

Albert and Dotsie were sitting on the sofa together, facing the front window, and Jonah could barely make out his girlfriend's words.

"Al, what happens when they catch you? Everyone is looking for you after what happened with Ms. Rose in court today. The sheriff is going to put you in jail. What will that do to us?"

The word 'us' took hold of Jonah's brain and he felt a surge of hate rocket through him. He looked at Margie and she appeared to want to vomit.

"Don't worry, love. They might put me in jail for a day or two but they will soon find out that Ms. Rose is mistaken, heck, she couldn't even see across this room much less out into a street where she could identify me. Jonah did it or had someone do it for him. It wasn't me, it was him and he killed Hunter too. They are going to convict him, mark my words, and we will be free to be together forever."

"I can't wait for the day, Al, when we can live here together. We can farm this place and you can be mayor. We can have a family here too."

The smile emanating from Albert Crenshaw could have lit up a thousand miles of countryside as pride and the sensation of victory took possession of him. He pulled Dotsie close for a kiss and she suddenly moved away.

"Albert, I'm really thirsty. I am going to get some lemonade from the kitchen...want some?"

Temporarily stymied, he nodded with a weaker smile.

"Yeah, Dotsie...I could use some lemonade too."

She moved through the dining area to the kitchen with hopes of making an escape but her captor was right behind her and she took note of the pistol in his hand, hanging at his side. Running was not an option.

"Margie." Jonah whispered to the girl at his side.

"Go back into town and get the sheriff. Do you know where he lives?"

"No, Jonah, I have no idea where he lives. Besides, I am not leaving Dotsie here with him...we can both stop him."

Jonah rolled his eyes, partially from the bravado that Margie was demonstrating and partially from disappointment that she could not get help.

"C'mon then, we are going in."

The pair quietly entered the house and hid in the entry alcove as they tried to calculate their next move. They didn't have much time to think because it wouldn't take long to pour two glasses of lemonade and they would probably return to the parlor. As expected, Albert and Dotsie reappeared and sat back down on the sofa.

As Dotsie turned to sit, she caught sight of Jonah and Margie and she almost dropped her lemonade. She could feel the blood pulsating in her head and the fear made her stammer as she tried to make small talk with Albert. Then she started to cry softly.

As Albert turned to comfort his lover, he suddenly saw a brown shoe sticking out from behind the alcove wall and he drew the pistol out in front of him. Dotsie sat back in shock.

"Whoever you are in the entryway, come out real slow or I will put some bullets in you. Move!"

Jonah and Margie appeared in the doorway and Albert let out a howling laugh.

"NO WAY….NO WAY… it's the DEVIL KID!"

"Don't you dare call him that! He's not the devil!"

Dotsie's declaration brought a sobering to Albert that signaled instant danger.

"You are standing up for him? For him? I thought you loved me! You still love him?"

The gun waived carelessly between the two friends standing ten feet away and the supposed lover on the sofa. Rage overcame the gunman.

"You two…get over here and sit down!" he barked as he rose to face the trio. He pointed the gun at Dotsie's face.

"You said you loved me! You said we could live here and we could have a family! Were you lying?"

His grip started to tighten on the weapon and he grimaced like a wild animal in a trap.

"You lied to me…you lied to me!"

Margie grabbed the glass of lemonade from the side table and flung it at Albert, hitting him in the head. He spun backwards with a yelp and the weapon discharged with a deafening sound, sending a bullet up into the ceiling.

Jonah attacked Albert, driving him to the floor and the gun flew backwards with a clatter. Both men scrambled toward the weapon and Albert was screaming with pain and rage as blood began to run down his forehead.

"RUN!" Jonah screamed as Albert crawled on top of him.

Both girls ran for the front door as fast as they could and began to cry as they realized that Jonah might need help. They heard both men scamper across the floor and tumble into a wall as they ran out of the front of the house. Ten steps away they turned to see Jonah coming out of the front door.

Albert appeared in the front doorway and leveled his weapon at the trio. He suddenly fell to the ground in a ragged heap. Sheriff Tom appeared on the porch and was now standing over the unconscious Albert. The lawman quickly knelt on the downed body and placed handcuffs to secure him.

The trio returned quickly to the lawman and began to explain what happened.

"Don't worry, I saw enough as you three ran off the porch. I figured I could handle him. Now, about you, Jonah. You could have ended up in a lot of trouble, possibly dead in there. What in the hell were you thinking? YOU WERE SUPPOSED TO STAY WITH ME AT ALL TIMES!"

Jonah's eyes and head dropped in a gesture of embarrassment and failure.

"I had to see Dotsie. I thought that she might be in trouble. I just had to go to her."

The sheriff said nothing in reply, he just gazed from the young man to his girlfriend, and then to the best friend with a look of disapproval.

"The three of you could have been killed tonight."

Chapter Thirty One

Albert Crenshaw sat in the basement of the courthouse, a shameful look of fear and despair blanketing his face. He knew he was in trouble; deep trouble and he didn't see a way out. The townspeople had built a sudden hatred and disdain toward him that he never bargained for.

"I am supposed to be the mayor here, the hero."

He muttered to himself, fearing the return of the judge and a new court case that would focus on him. One week from now he would be on trial and things would really fall apart. The young man began to cry as he realized his plans with Dotsie would never be realized. He would probably go to prison for a long time and might even be executed. Maybe that would be better than life imprisonment. Certainly better than trying to live in this hateful community.

Three large men appeared at the door to his cell. They were dressed in ornate suits with dark, dapper hats and they looked much too strong to challenge.

"Get up and get dressed, you are coming with us."

Fear flooded the young man's mind.

"Where? Where are we going? Why are we leaving?" he stammered with fear.

"Just quiet down and come with us."

Albert now looked frantically for assistance and realized that the sheriff was nowhere to be found.

Rising to street level, he was led out of the back door of the courthouse and the bright sun stung his eyes, forcing him to close them as he moved to an automobile nearby. Two of the men pushed him into the back seat and the third got behind the steering wheel.

"Where are we going?" he asked again in a panic.

"Shut up and sit still. Do not make us use a gag on you. Do not make us kill you."

The automobile pulled up to the park and slowly came to a stop near the pavilion in the middle. The men grabbed Albert and moved him into the structure where they tied him to a post and placed a gag in his mouth. It was now that the young man began to bawl and shake convulsively. He knew what his outcome would be...how his story would end.

The parade assembled on the north side of town, just out of view of the main street. The young man was taken to the end of the line and placed atop the last float. As he sat up high, he felt a wave of celebrity status and familiarity rush over him. The people in front of him turned around to face him while calling out his name. The overzealous parade members were just the beginning of the show of affection that would be tossed his way when the whole group would move slowly along the actual parade route. The celebration just heightened his sense of being and belonging.

The participants turned around and began their steady march on the route. The police car leading the group turned on to Main

Street and the noise grew louder as the townspeople recognized the beginning of the event. The street was lined with three people deep on both sides and little kids sitting on the curb with hopes of getting plenty of attention and candy thrown at them from the marchers. A small but boisterous high school band followed Sheriff Tom's squad car and patriotic songs now filled the air. Jonah's float was at the end of the parade because he was the honored one.

Smiling and waving to all he could see, the young man soon realized that the event and celebrity status accorded him was reaching a finality. Sadness overcame him as he realized the fun would soon end but he pushed it to the back of his mind, determined to enjoy every last second of the celebration.

With a final cheer and wave to the crowd the destination of the procession had come into sight. The beautiful little park with the wooden pavilion sat off to his right and everyone gathered around it. Jonah had been here before. A proud smile crossed his face as he was helped off the wagon and led to picnic tables that held more food than he had ever seen.

Led to the head of the largest table, he soon became aware of his fellow guests. The people around him treated him like their long-lost son. He thought for a quick moment and concluded that this could be the best day of his life.

The food was provided at his table and he made a conscious effort to not to wolf it down and look like a slob. As carefully as he could, Jonah took his time and tried to show proper manners as he ate plate after plate. The aroma and taste were dynamic, again it was the best food that he could recall having. The banquet came to a slow but satisfying end with toasts to Jonah by the most prominent guests.

The crowd of hundreds now gathered in front of the small pavilion and quickly moved Jonah to the front of the group. After checking to make sure a bullet was in the chamber, the rifle was handed to Jonah carefully with great ceremonial ritual. He looked down at the weapon and realized that it could have very well ended his life months before. He shivered slightly as he moved his focus to the closed window in front of him.

One person stood to the right of Albert and another to the left. Both backed away and the young man began to cry out, his plea for his life muffled by a rag stuffed into his mouth. The small window opened and through tears he recognized Jonah pointing a rifle at him from twenty yards away. Urine ran down his leg and his pants filled as his body let go of all control.

Jonah aimed the rifle carefully at his target. He then turned to the crowd and set the weapon down carefully at his feet. The crowd went from cheering to silence in an instant.

"A couple of months ago that was me, Jonah Edwards, standing in that window. Hunter Carlyle stood here with a rifle. I was about to become an innocent victim of a terrible ritual, one that is senseless and cruel. I recognize that our town once saw this as an important tradition that moves a person from childhood to adulthood. It is time we found a new way, a more humane way. In the time I have been here I have grown to love so much about this town, about you people. We are all too good for this. From this day onward I ask you to end this senselessness. We are so much better than this."

The crowd said nothing, letting the words permeate their consciousness. Then a voice came from the group, strong yet with respect.

"Are we to let him go? After all that he has done? He needs to face his punishment."

Nods and whispers of agreement followed the voice. Sheriff Tom raised his voice with authority.

"He will get the proper consequences for his actions when Judge Clark comes back to town for court next week. Albert is not going anywhere. There are three federal marshals always guarding him. I am watching him as well. He will get what he deserves when the right time comes. I will personally make sure of that."

Jonah turned to face Albert, who looked like he was in shock and already half dead. Then he turned back to the people.

"We should continue to celebrate in our community. Let's create something new, something we can be proud of. We are too good for this."

Clapping started in the back, slowly and lightly and then gained in intensity as it grew closer to the guest of honor. Dotsie moved to her lover and they engaged in a long, passionate kiss as the crowd roared its approval. The ritual was dead and a new one would take its place.

Chapter Thirty Two

"But grandma, what happened to the bad guy, to Albert?"

The old lady paused and looked out across the lawn to the road in front of the farmstead, then off in the distance. The air was still, and rain clouds were forming over the hot, humid, shimmering green field of corn far beyond.

"He went away for a very long time."

The little blonde girl is suddenly confused and it shows on her expression. She pauses for a moment and then looks back up at her grandmother.

"Where did he go?"

"A place called Leavenworth, a long way from here, so you don't have to worry about him. The bad man is gone. What do you say we get grandpa to take a break and join us for some lemonade."

The young girl smiled and turned toward the front yard as her grandmother called out in a sweet, loving voice.

"Jonah, come on over here and have some lemonade with us."

The old man slowly turned and gazed across the yard, his eyes stopping at the meadow that he had encountered so many years ago. His studious gaze continued to move with his weathered body and finally rested on the woman who had saved his life. Jonah muttered to himself as he moved to the porch and a gentle smile formed on his face.

"This could be the best day of my life."

The End

Acknowledgments

This work would not have been possible without the help and encouragement of so many people. Special thanks go out to Ashlyn Callison and April Sundstrom, who took so much of their own time to read, edit, and critique this story. Without their assistance this novel would fall short in style and narrative. My lovely wife Sarah, sacrificed quality time with me and put up with my questioning of the story line on long drives to the lake. My family also made sure to leave me the time to work on this novel and I hold value in their patience and wisdom. Finally, thank you to all the people who have encouraged me to write another book, you have supported me and my passion for writing and I will always be grateful.

About The Author

D.J. Hamlin is a published writer through Northern Star Publishing and "The Best Day Of His Life" is his fifth novel. In addition to his latest work, the author has also written a thrilling spy series that includes "The Middle Man", "Half A World Away", and "Shooter". These feature the fictional spy character named Brian Konrad. When he is not writing, D.J. teaches Social Studies and coaches football in the beautiful state of Minnesota.

Other Works by D.J. Hamlin

The Middle Man, The Brian Konrad Series, Book One. A Minneapolis museum curator has a dark secret to hide during the 1950's Cold War. Is it possible to escape one's past?

Half A World Away, The Brian Konrad Series, Book Two. Can Brian Konrad evade the United States Government while hiding a Half a World Away?

Shooter, The Brian Konrad Series, Book 3. A new challenge presents itself in a new era as a Soviet leader makes a famed visit to the U.S. A plot is uncovered that could change world leadership and the hierarchy of power across the world.

"Stand Up and Cheer: 75 Years of Packer Hockey" A history of the famed high school hockey program in South St. Paul, Minnesota.

"Transplant", A teen gets a new lease on life with a partial brain transplant, only to realize that there is now a middle-aged man in his head with a mystery to solve.